DEAD RECKONING

A Short Story Collection

Mary Ann Back

Grey Wolfe Publishing, LLC
PO Box 1088
Birmingham, Michigan 48009
www.GreyWolfePublishing.com

© 2015 Mary Ann Back
Cover design by TheCoverCounts.com
Published by Grey Wolfe Publishing, LLC
www.GreyWolfePublishing.com
All Rights Reserved

FIRST EDITION ISBN: 978-1628280760
SECOND EDITION ISBN: 978-1628281491

Library of Congress Control Number: 2015935170

Grey Wolfe Publishing LLC
Lú bóna na coróin

Dead Reckoning

A Short Story Collection

Mary Ann Back

Dedication

I dedicate this anthology to Dr. Mark Helmick, my eighth-grade English teacher, who first inspired me to write. Thank you for your encouragement. It led me to my true passion in life.

And thank you to Harper Lee, whose novel, "To Kill A Mockingbird", forever reminds me that the key to a spellbinding story is, plot, heart, and voice.

Contents

A Different Shade Of Death

Henri Leon made a fine looking corpse. Everybody said so. Still, we didn't admire him too long. Bodies turn south of cheese quick in the Luzianna heat.

The band struck up a dirge, and we took Henri to a crypt on the northeast side of St. Sebastian Cemetery. After a proper reading from the Good Book and a respectable show of tears, the dirge gave way to the joyful noise of Cajun jazz that leads the dead to their final reward; and the living to the closest bar.

Aside from the fact that Henri wasn't truly dead, it was one hell of a send-off. And to be fair, in the bayou, sometimes it's hard to know when dead is really dead. Down here, there's a different shade of death. It was Lamont Braxton who made Henri dead and Mammie Odette who made him undead. I know 'cause I saw it all.

And, even though, that cemetery was hotter than the flames of perdition, a chill slithered up my spine. I knew what night would bring. I left St. Sebastian's whispering, "Be seeing you, Henri. Just remember, we was friends." That's true enough.

But Henri and Lamont, now there were two souls destined to collide.

＊＊＊＊

Henri and Lamont loved the same woman, Ophelia, daughter of Mammie Odette. But Henri beat Lamont to the punch and popped the question.   No one was surprised when Ophelia said yes.

Henri was a catch and Ophelia is just about the prettiest gal in Terrebonne Parish.   Tiny as a hummingbird, she is, with eyes the color of the ocean.   Her gumbo can make a grown man weep.

Mammie, well Mammie took me and Henri in when we wasn't much bigger than tadpoles. Orphans we were, livin' on the streets and eatin' out of garbage cans. That upset Mammie's sensibilities.   She's as round as a whiskey barrel and not a whole lot taller.   She's a powerful woman who can sing a babe to sleep or summon hellfire.   She was mighty fond of Henri.   So was I.

The night Henri died he and Ophelia was sitting in Mammie's parlor spinning big dreams and making plans like lovers do. Mammie was teaching me about herbs and such.   We moved to the back room pulling the long purple curtain across the doorway to give them some privacy.   Everything was right as rain 'til the door burst open, and Ophelia screamed.

Mammie and I jumped up.   She motioned for me to hush. We peeked out from behind the curtain and saw Lamont pulling a bloody knife from Henri's heart.

"Teach you to steal what's mine, Henri Leon!   Rot in hell, you stinkin' thief!" screamed Lamont.   Poor Henri was dead before he hit the floor.

 Mammie charged Lamont, and he lunged at her with the knife.   But her eyes rolled back in her head, so all I could see was

---

white. Conjurin' up a power I'd never seen before, she lifted her hand straight out in front of her and shouted, "I bind you from me!" A beam of bright light rose between them. No matter how he moved, Lamont couldn't get to her through that light.

Mammie grabbed for a small canister from the pantry shelf and dumped its yellow powder into her hand. "You's a murderer, Lamont Braxton!" she shrieked, "But hear me, it ain't over between you and Henri. Not just yet." She leaned over Henri, blew the powder in his face and cried, "When you hear me call, Henri, you shall rise!"

Lamont looked like he'd just seen the second coming, and I wasn't sure he hadn't.   He dropped the knife and took off runnin'. But I'd heard that spell Mammie laid on Henri. I understood what it meant. I knew I'd be seeing both those boys again real soon.

And Lamont was smart to run.

****

At midnight, after Henri was laid to rest, Mammie and I returned to the cemetery. The day's heat rose from the ground and hovered like ghosts dancin' in the moonlight. Sounds I'd never heard before filled the air—moans and shrieks came from the dead who wanted no part in what we was about to do. Mammie stretched out her arms toward the crypt, held her head high and bellowed, "Come to me, Henri!   Awaken, child! Vengeance is yours!"

Didn't Henri rise from that crypt!   Lookin' like Henri, but not. It was his eyes. There was nobody home behind those eyes. He started walkin', and we started followin' all the way to Kitchamee Swamp. That's where we found Lamont curled up on the bank, hiding beneath a blanket of wet mud, crying like a baby.

My blood ran cold as Henri jerked him out of that swamp like a sack of corn. "God have mercy on your soul, Lamont!" I prayed.   But God wasn't in Kitchamee that night.   Just Henri – undead Henri – who proceeded to claw his way through flesh and bone snatching Lamont's still-beating heart right out of his chest!

Lamont's body won't never be found.   The swamp don't give up its dead.

Mammie took Henri by the hand and led him back to the crypt.   With tears on her cheeks, she laid him down, brushed her hand over his eyes and said, "You did well, Henri.   Vengeance is done.   Sleep well, child.   I won't be callin' you again."

I believed her.

****

I took some pretty white oleander to Henri today and visited for a time.   Thinkin' on everything that happened.   Tryin' to make sense of it all.

I reckoned I'd glimpsed that gray space between life and death, where what could never be, is—where the dead walk and can finish unfinished business.   I'd glimpsed that different shade of death.

Aces and Alibis

I always knew how to piss Tommy off. He said that was my one true talent. But then we'd make love, and he'd say okay, maybe I had two. But that was then, and this was now.

"Trip bullets? You draw trip bullets and think you're leaving with my 10G's in your pocket? That ain't happening, Dottie. One more hand." Christ, but his face was purple.

I know when the lamb's been fleeced enough.

"Schedule's a little tight, Tommy. I got a date with Louie." I blew my Lucky in his face and turned on my heel.

"You ain't going nowhere, Sweetheart." His fingers dug into my arm like ticks digging into a dog.

We were in the V.I.P. room of The Oasis Lounge, which was technically the storeroom any other day of the week. Tommy, my ex, owned this dive, from the peeling plaster walls to the leaky john in the ladies' room. He won it from Dominick Ferretti in a lucky hand of poker. Tommy liked it when the stakes were high.

We started playing Draw Poker around suppertime, five knuckleheads and me. One by one, they took their sad sack faces and empty pockets home. By two in the morning, Tommy and I were the only ones left. I'd played fair and square up to then. I know my cards. But I was done taking chances. I opened a new deck, telling Tommy it was to keep him honest. I swapped it for the spare deck that was sitting on the table when he went to the can. The new deck matched the aces up my sleeve. When he came back, we played that ten-thousand-dollar hand—the one with the trip bullets. That might have been overkill, but it felt good. Revenge usually does. Judging by the look on Tommy's face, I'd hit him where it hurt.

I needed an out, so I said, "Time to call it a night, Tommy. All the guys went home, and you and me, we ain't playing slap and tickle anymore. Ciao."

He grabbed my arm. "Hey, let go! Don't be such a sore loser. You're hurting me!"

"Sit down!" His voice blew like a bullhorn but, he let go of me.

"You don't look so good," I said. "Your face is all sweaty and your eye's twitchy. Where's your blood pressure pill? I'll get you some water." I broke for the door, but he blocked me.

"Nice try, Dottie."

"I gotta go. Louie's expecting me."

"We'll cut cards. Double or nothing—high card takes all. Then you and Louie can slap each other silly if you want."

"Fine," I said, grabbing for the deck, but his fist came down with a bang.

"No way, Toots. Give 'em here."

"Why should you cut?"

"On account of I don't trust you."

"Yeah? Well, you tried to screw my daughter. I win." I snaked the cards out from under his meatball hand and said, "Let's do this. I got places to be." The memory of seeing his hands on my Cheri got my blood boiling.

He let go of the deck, but his eyes were glued to it – like they used to be glued to me.

The cards inside my right sleeve jiggled. I'd been begging for this night, for the right combination of guts and timing. He needed to lose what he loved most. And I was going to be the one to take it from him. I slipped one of those aces into that deck slick as you please and turned my cut face up.

"Well, would you look at that ace?" I asked.

The table went flying, and Tommy grabbed me by my hair. "You lousy bitch! How many more cards you got up there?" He threw one arm around my neck and reached up my sleeve with the other. A fifth ace fluttered to the floor. "Jesus, how many bullets do you need to win? Christ, if you ain't a dumb broad!" He clocked my jaw and sent me sailing across the room on my backside.

When I looked up, he was coming at me with the shiv he kept tucked in his boot. I scrambled to my feet and pointed my left hand straight at his heart. The .22 inside my sleeve popped like a firecracker and bright red splotch spread across his shirt.

"That's for Cheri," I said.

He groaned and dropped his knife, then staggered backward, and slumped to the floor, looking at me like he couldn't believe his eyes. His last words were, "Damn Baby, what else you got in that jacket?"

I put on some lipstick, checked my hair, and sucked back the rest of my martini. It was time to blow that joint and head to Louie's. Slipping on my gloves, I went to step over Tommy, but something stopped me. I guess I figured I owed him a few words on account of were close once.   So I bent down, picked the money up off the floor, and whispered in his ear, "You always were the smart one, Baby. Oh, and about me not needing all those bullets to win? Looks like you were right about that, too. Turns out, I only needed one."

So much for goodbyes. I snatched the money from the cash register and his wallet, too. It wasn't like he was going to be using it. Besides, somebody came in and robbed poor Tommy before he had a chance to lock up for the night. It wouldn't make sense to leave the dough behind.

I walked out into the snow-covered street and left the door wide open. This end of town, there wouldn't be a single bottle of hooch left by morning and the cops would find more footprints inside than they could on Main Street. I watched the fog swirl under the streetlight and thought about Louie, gullible, love-struck Louie who'd sell his soul to protect me and my 'talents'. Right about now, he'd be warming up my side of the bed in the classiest house on Cherry Street, listening for me to come through the door. I turned my collar against the cold and picked up my pace. It's not smart to leave an alibi waiting.

Away

      Molly Porter vanished from Willow Grove in the spring of 2011. Search parties searched, and prayer circles prayed. Her name peppered the public over every radio station and in every headline for weeks. Not that it made any difference. When spring gave way to the dog days of summer, Molly's fifteen minutes of fame faded like a sun-bleached newspaper. Prayers morphed into stares, and the gossiping magpies of Willow Grove ripped Molly to pieces, as surely as if they'd scavenged her body in the middle of Main Street. Devastated, Molly's mother, Ruth, disappeared into a bottle of Tennessee's finest. From time to time, I've been known to join her there.

      I'm Tyler Finnegan, better known as Finn to my friends. To those few who are in no danger of ever being considered my friends, I am simply Finnegan.   I was born and raised in Willow Grove, home of the aforementioned chin-waggers. Having no shortage of dirty laundry myself, I allow mine to flap in the breeze for all to see. Withholding fodder from the magpies drives them crazy.

Small southern towns churn gossip like butter. They seldom let facts get in the way of the truth. Ugly rumors, dark innuendoes, and wild-ass theories about Molly's disappearance ran rampant. She did the entire Willow Grove football team and ran off in disgrace. She hitched a ride cross-country with a long-haul trucker. And my personal favorite, she was abducted by aliens at Miller's Pond.

Speculation blows, but at least it blows with the wind. So in September of 2011, when Councilman Cranley was indicted for embezzlement, the magpies, craving fresh meat, swarmed their newest victim and left the gnawed bones of Molly's disappearance to rot like yesterday's road kill. That's when Molly took on an odd, almost mystical quality.

Folks in Willow Grove stopped referring to her as missing. Instead, they'd say, she was away. Away as in simply, not here. Ipso facto, she might, or might not return, if and when she was damned good and ready. Once the town succeeded in burying its collective head up its narrow-minded ass, secure in its belief that no child could be forcibly ripped from our little slice of heaven, parents stopped hovering over their children like helicopters and visualizing their tiny faces on milk cartons. Panic subsided, life began to return to normal, and by Thanksgiving, 2011, all that remained of Molly Porter was a weathered poster stapled to some telephone poles.

Away might have let the people of Willow Grove move on, but not Molly's mother. And not me.

Every day at Louie's, I'd order the same lunch—a double Tanqueray, neat. I'd toss back some bar nuts and drift into a trance, rehashing facts I'd poured over a thousand times before. Old Louie would catch me staring out through the nicotine haze at Main Street.

He'd say, "Finn, you gotta let it go." He'd wipe down the bar, looking like he wanted to say something more, but thought better of it. He'd chew on it for a while, and then unable to contain himself, spit out his shiny if obscure, pearl of wisdom. "She amscrayed, that's all, kid. She's just a skirt who got herself in dutch with some mook and flew the coup."

Louie's hardboiled pearls could always bring me out of my trance. "Once again, in English, please," I'd say. Louie was seventy-five, maybe pushing eighty and came from the age of film noir. I was nearing thirty and born with a USB port instead of a belly button. Louie and I were lucky if we understood each other half the time. "Why should I let it go?" I'd ask him. "It's not like I've got another case to work on." Louie would shrug his shoulders and commiserate with me in the universal language of Bartender by pouring me another double.

The town of Willow Grove was about two blinks long. There wasn't enough work to keep an enterprising private eye busy, so I made ends meet running background checks for employers. I'd have moved on to more promising towns bloated with sin and vice if it weren't for the mystery of Molly.

She was eighteen when she disappeared. She used to clean my office on Friday's after school. Sweet kid. Said she was saving up for college—roped me in for $25 a week. I figured, what the hell. She worked cheap, and I was a soft touch. Nice mom, she had, too. Single. Hard-working. When I told her I'd find Molly, I meant it. After her mom went into exile, I used to stop by her place once a week, to check up on her, then it dropped to every couple weeks, until finally, I realized I was creating reasons not to go. Three years had gone by since Molly disappeared. It was getting harder to look her mother in the eye. But I'd made her a promise. Come a day, this case would break wide open. And I'd be the one doing the breaking.

The day that happened was June 25, 2014, and Dewey Wilson's tow truck rumbled past the bar, hauling a mud-covered '95 Cutlass.

"Jesus!" I shouted, knocking over my stool, and scrambling out the door. Dewey was sitting at the red light at 8th and Main. The winched up car hanging from the back of his truck oozed wet mud. I zeroed in on its back window. Bingo. Underneath the sludge was a patch of yellow from the smiley face sticker I knew was there. "Dewey! Hey Dewey, hold up!" I yelled. No one was behind him, so he idled at the light, waiting for me.

"What's up?" he asked.

"You know whose car that is? Was anybody in it?"

"Naw. Chief Pickett just called and asked me to pull it out of Miller's pond. Said Will Bailey's fishing line snagged it. Whose is it?"

"Never mind. I'm coming up." I climbed up onto the truck and edged my way back to the Cutlass.

"Hey! Get off! I gotta haul this to impound, Chief's orders." Dewey squirmed in his seat. "This is evidence. You're gonna get me fired, man. C'mon."

"Just give me a minute, that's all I need. One minute. Light a smoke or something," I stuck my head through the open passenger window. It stunk like week-old fish. I leaned inside so far that I was hanging by my waist on the door. Something was sticking up through the muck on the floorboard. I didn't know what it was, but I wanted it. Just then, Chief Pickett's voice blared through the window.

"Dewey, what the hell are you doing? Didn't I tell you to take that car to impound? And whose ass is sticking out of that window?"

"That's Finn, Chief."

I yanked what I'd seen out of the muck, shoved it into my jacket pocket, and wiggled back out. "Morning, Officer Pickett," I said, just to piss him off.

"That's Chief Pickett to you, son. Get down off my evidence." I did as I was told. "Did you take anything from inside there?" he asked.

"No, sir," I said, "That'd be illegal."

"Uh huh."

"Go ahead, search me if you want." I was covered with pond scum and reeked liked spoiled fish guts.

"Get out of here, Finnegan. We'll handle this. The day I need help from a private investigator, I'll give you a call—maybe next stick-your-thumb-up-your-ass day."

Dick-wad. He'd been chief since '94. Pickett couldn't find his johnson with a flashlight, let alone Molly Porter. But somehow he always managed to get re-elected. He was so far up Mayor Larkin's ass; you'd need barbecue tongs and a headlamp to pull him out.

I walked back to the bar to suck down the rest of my lunch. I hadn't seen Louie look so animated in years. He didn't know whether to scratch his watch or wind his ass.

"Was that...?"

"Molly Porter's car? Yeah." I said, slamming down my empty shot glass and heading back out the door.

Louie hollered after me, "Watch your keister, hear me? You go picking a fight with a dog, be sure you got the bigger bite."

There was a message somewhere in that randomness. I got to my office and emptied my pocket onto the desk—car keys, forty-three cents, a half pack of Rolaids, and something caked in mud. I scraped off most of the dirt and saw that it was a drink token from the Rusty Bucket out on Barrett Road—Ben Watson's place. Old Ben didn't know it yet, but he and I were going to have a chat.

****

I hadn't been to the Rusty Bucket in years. Nothing much had changed, except Ben. He looked like a bag of bones. I wondered if he'd even remember me.

"Finn! I'll be damned. Haven't seen you in a coon's age. Tanqueray, right?" He smiled and filled a shot glass to the rim. I suddenly remembered why I used to drink there. "What brings you to my neck of the woods?" he asked.

"Molly Porter."

His smiled flickered a little. "Molly Porter? Haven't heard that name in years." He poured some stale beer nuts in a bowl. "She's gone. Ran off a few years back, if I remember."

"She ever come in here, Ben?"

"Heck, she was just a kid, Finn."

"She was eighteen. Ever see her in here?" He didn't answer, just shrugged and wiped down the bar. That made me think of Louie, and I laughed.

"What's so funny?" he asked.

"You bartenders. Why is it that when you don't know what to say, you start wiping down the bar?"

He laid down the rag and leaned in close. "What can I do for you, son?"

"Was Molly Porter ever in here?" I slid the muddy drink token across the bar. He didn't even look at it.

"Let it go, Finn."

"Damn it, Ben! A minute ago you told me she ran off. Now you're telling me to let it go. What aren't you telling me?" I picked up the token and held it in front of his face. "Want to know where this came from? Out of her car. Dewey Wilson fished her Cutlass out of Miller's Pond today. So I'm going to ask you one more time. Was Molly Porter ever in here?"

He paused with a sigh and stared out the window. "Once. She was only in here once—the night she went missing. Sat right over there." He pointed to the corner booth next to the jukebox.

"Who was she with?" I asked.

"Hard to say. That was a long time ago."

"You're sharp as a tack, Ben. You even remembered what I drink, and I haven't been here in close to ten years." I took off my jacket and opened a menu. "I'm not leaving till you tell me."

He shoved some Luckys into the cigarette rack. "I give you a name; this place is liable to burn to the ground. Or I'll end up running off the road some night after closing. Get my drift?"

"We never talked. Just give me a name."

He stared at his feet and said, "Chief Pickett."

Shit. Any name but his.

"Pickett? What was she doing here with Pickett?"

"I swear, I don't know. I didn't want to know. They talked, he looked mad; she started crying. Next thing I know, he's dragging her out by her arm."

When I left, Ben looked even older than when I'd walked in. Pickett. The bastard. That explained a lot. No wonder the cops never found Molly. Whatever Pickett had to do with this, his ass was mine.

Molly's Cutlass was locked in impound; I wasn't going to get a second look at it. Besides, Pickett would have ditched any evidence from inside it by now. That car had been sitting on the bottom of Miller's Pond with its passenger window open for three years. What were the odds there might be something else floating in that pond besides algae? Like something from inside her car. It didn't matter what it was—anything that could help me find Molly. I was going for a swim.

****

Daylight was all but gone. The water was dirty. I could see where Dewey's tow truck had backed up to the edge of the pond. That didn't mean that Molly's car entered the water there, but it was a place to start. I stripped down to my skivvies and spent maybe fifteen minutes bobbing up and down, looking like a blind squirrel chasing an acorn. My teeth were chattering, and I was losing feeling in my hands. A wetsuit would have been useful. I was ready to move on to Plan B, and I didn't even have one. Being a seat-of-the-pants kind of guy, I find that working under pressure suits me. Plan B would be popping out any minute, so I crawled out of the pond, freezing, and mumbling a random assortment of four letter words. That's when I got clobbered from behind and went down for the count.

I'm not sure how long I was out. Waking up with a mouthful of dirt and a knot the size of a walnut on the back of my head brought forth an even louder round of profanity. Other than the sound of croaking frogs, it was quiet. I rolled over to find some big-ass footprints in the mud alongside me, way bigger than my feet would make, then I raised my eyes to the blanket of stars in the sky and groaned. If somebody'd wanted to kill me, I'd have woken up dead. No, this goose egg had been a message, loosely translated, 'Back off'. Message received loud and clear. The problem was; I didn't give a rat's ass. I wasn't throwing in the towel. Not now. I wobbled to my feet like a drunken sailor, arms and legs slipping and sliding out from beneath me until I landed face first in the willow grass. There, not two inches in front of my nose, nestled among the reeds, was a wet, swollen leather wallet.

It could have belonged to anyone, really. If I'd have searched through the weeds long enough, I could have probably found car keys, belts, a complete Tupperware collection, not to mention an assortment of unmentionables. A picnicker might have left the wallet behind. Some kid from town could have lost it during a moonlight skinny dip. Or maybe, just maybe, it might have washed out of Molly's car when the wrecker hauled it out. That wasn't possible, I told myself, not after all the time that had gone by; and as water-logged as it was, would anything in it be useful. I scooped it up anyway, got dressed, and shoved it into the pocket of my jeans. I wanted it to believe it was Molly's, even if once it was opened, my heart would sink.

Fighting the urge to barf, I climbed back into my Mazda and hoped my vision would clear. When I finally pulled back onto Skillet Lick Road, I instinctively took the wallet out of my jeans. Someone knew I was poking around on this case. If it was Molly's wallet, it needed to be kept safe. I knew just where to put it. I reached under the driver' seat and shoved it up inside, deep in the springs, next to the Glock I keep hidden there—just in case.

Navigating Skillet Lick Road, with its twists and turns, is a challenge on any summer night, when the warmth of a sunny afternoon swirls off the pavement in a wall of fog. My double vision added icing to the cake. If I hadn't been so focused on the curves in front of me, I might have seen the flashing lights gaining on me from behind. When the siren whooped, I knew who it was. Most of me wanted to flip him the bird and take my chances in the fog, but the little dude in the back of my brain, the one that keeps me alive despite my grandest plans, bitch-slapped me back into reality. I pulled over and remembered the Glock under my seat—just in case.

I rolled down the window with a smile. "Evening, Officer Pickett." Those few occasions, when I do manage to slip something past the little guy in my brain, never seem to end well.

"Why do you do that, Finnegan?" he asked

"What?"

He jammed his nightstick into my gullet. "Intentionally irritate the piss out of me?"

"It's a gift."

He gave his nightstick an extra shove, and then removed it from my throat. "Punk." His flashlight scanned the inside of my car. "You were weaving back there. I'm going to have to search your vehicle. You don't have any problem with that, right?"

"By all means, please. Good thing I sold all my dope yesterday or that could have been ugly."

"Step out of the car. Stand right there, where I can see you. No funny stuff."

It was hard enough for me to find my hiding spot inside the driver's seat. I was willing to bet he wouldn't. Like I had a choice. While he rummaged through my car, I stood in his line of sight like a good boy and stared off-road, wondering how lucky he'd be. When he came up snake eyes, I smirked, and it pissed him off even more. He stood nose to nose with me.

"Where you been, boy?" he growled.

"Just taking a drive, sir."

He glanced at the blood on my collar, followed it up to the lump on my head, and grinned. "What happened there?" He tapped the knot with his nightstick.

"Shit!" I grabbed his stick before my little brain dude could stop me. Pickett went straight for my windpipe, pinched it tight, and slammed my head down on the open window track.

"You ain't too bright, are you, boy?"

"What do you want?" I wheezed.

"I want you to be careful, Finnegan. That's what I want. Listen to me good. There are folks in this town who don't want you sniffing where you shouldn't be sniffing. Digging up things don't need to see the light of day. You could get hurt. Or worse. Now go home, before you do something we'll all regret."

He let go of my throat. I crumpled to the ground with my head against the door guard, its rubber strip, gouging a dent into the side of my face. Which folks in town had secrets that needed keeping—folks that Pickett gave a rat's ass about? Willow Grove was a flyspeck of a town. The list had to be short. For the second time that night, my legs tried to gather beneath me but weren't up to the task. I sucked in air, watched him strut back to his cruiser, and listened to the thud of his steps on the pavement. I couldn't help but notice the clumps of wet mud sticking to the bottom of his big-ass boots.

****

After a long, hot shower, I poured myself a double and placed a package of frozen corn on my goose egg. Mom always said to use peas, dad swore by corn; me, I think the only thing that works is Tanqueray—in massive doses.

I placed the pink clutch style wallet on the kitchen table and unzipped it. One by one, I laid its contents out on the grey, Formica top—a gift card to Shiloh's Tasty Freeze, four singles, and a movie pass. My heart raced when I turned over a driver's license. It was Molly's. The random collection of cards and papers that had been shoved into the bill section of the wallet were ruined by the water and impossible to read. There were a few pictures in the plastic photo sleeves that had fared a little better, one of her mom and one of her best friend, Lena Bowers. My mouth went dry when I found one of Molly and me standing next to her Cutlass on the day she bought it. She and her mom stopped by the office to show it off. Her mom insisted on me being in the picture. Said Molly couldn't have bought it without me giving her a job. I teased the wet picture from the plastic sleeve and put it on my mantle. I thought Molly would approve. In fact, it almost seemed like fate, or Molly, had stepped in—as if the picture had been biding its time, waiting for me in the weeds. Like she put it there because she knew I'd find it. Tucked tight behind that picture was a business card from The King County Women's Center, in Highpoint, the next town over. I could still read the appointment date on the card. It was May 5, 2011. The day before Molly went missing.

I threw back another double, hell, it was more like three fingers and swallowed a couple of Tylenol for good measure. I lay there, eyes closed, in the dark, thinking about the life that Molly never had the chance to live.

****

Daylight arrived, and a vague thumping in my head awakened me. Unsure whether it was from the Tanqueray or the goose egg, I experimented with a curative blend of black coffee and two more Tylenol. I sat at the kitchen table, working the crossword puzzle, chain smoking Marlboros, and watching one of those early morning excuses for a news show, the ones where the host's smiles are decoupaged onto their botoxed faces. I drained the coffee pot, and then my bladder, and counted down the seconds until ten o'clock. According to the card in Molly's wallet, that's the time The King County Women's Center opened. There was no way I'd get any personal information about Molly from a phone call. But it was a place to start. My fingers shook when I tapped the number into my cell phone. That might have been caused by nerves, or it might have been a remnant of the Tanqueray. Hard to tell. The call connected.

"King County Women's Center. How may I help you?"

The voice on the line sounded young. Good. "Hi, this is Jim Hensel, from the King County Better Business Bureau. With whom am I speaking?"

"Amanda Cook."

"Amanda, we're updating our corporate directory and need a moment of your time to outline the services you provide for the community."

"Just a moment, please, I'll connect you to Ms. Shoenberger, our office manager."

"No, no need to disturb the office manager, Amanda. I'm sure she's a busy lady, and the information I need is very basic. Tell me when you're ready."

"Sure." I could hear her tapping her pen on the desk. "What did you need?"

"Just tell me about the services you provide at the center."

"We are a judgment-free facility devoted to women's sexual health, providing a full range of planned parenthood services, including sexually transmitted disease testing and prenatal care."

Straight from the pamphlet, no doubt, but exactly what I needed. Pick one—STD or baby. My heart sank. "Thank you for your time, Amanda. You were most helpful. Have a great day."

"You too, sir."

I glanced again at the picture of Lena Bowers. When it came to Molly and Lena, you never saw one without the other. They were two peas until Molly went missing. In short order, Lena moved to Highpoint and went to work in a tiny beauty salon called, Rock, Paper, Scissors.

If you were a pregnant teenager, wouldn't you confide in your bestie? I felt a sudden urge for a haircut.

****

Frankly, Lena had reason to be suspicious of me from the moment I entered her shop. "A little off the top. Not too much, now. It's taken thirty years to rock this look." I slid my hand over my head and preened a little.

She pursed her lips and raised her eyebrows. "Suppose you tell me why you're really here?" The canned lighting from the ceiling glared off my bald head.

"I'm Finn," I said as if that explained everything.

"I know who you are. I asked why you're here."

"I want to talk about Molly Porter."

She turned away, grabbed her broom and began sweeping up the hair on the floor. After thinking for a moment, she said, "Molly left town."

"Where is she?"

"Away. How should I know?"

"You were her best friend."

"And?"

"And you know more than you're telling me." I grabbed hold of the broom. "Where is she?" She tried to walk away, but I caught her wrist.

"That was a long time ago, Mr. Finnegan. Don't go dragging me back there." There was a haunted look about her, the look of someone who's kept a secret too long.

"What are you afraid of, Lena? Just tell me what you know, and I'll protect you, I swear."

Her eyes welled up. "Let me make this easy for you," I said. "She was pregnant and seeing the doctors at the King County Women's Center." I took her hands in mine. "Who was the father?"

She bolted like a wild horse. "You need to leave—now." She opened the door to the shop and stared me out of my chair and out to the sidewalk. I was so damn close to the truth I could taste it.

"This isn't right, Lena. She was your friend." I stepped off the sidewalk toward my car.

"Mr. Finnegan?" she called. I turned around, not daring to breathe. "It was Troy Larkin's baby. And her appointment at that clinic? It wasn't for prenatal care. She was getting an abortion, but she changed her mind and cancelled the appointment."

For a moment, the world stopped spinning. Troy Larkin, the mayor's son. Jesus. A shit storm was about to blow. All I could manage to say was, "Thanks for doing the right thing."

****

I climbed back into my car and looked at the clock. It was noon, a two-hour drive to Knoxville. Troy was a running back at the University of Tennessee. Go Volunteers! *Tick tock, Troy Boy. I'm coming. Your all-conference ass can run, but it can't hide.*

Finding Troy was easy. Everyone knew Troy. I knocked on the door to his dorm room, figuring that he wouldn't be in. He opened the door, and a fog of weed wafted into my face. "Hi Troy. I'm Finn, from Willow Grove. Got a minute?" I didn't wait for an invitation; I breezed right past him into the room.

"Yeah, I know who you are," he said. "What do you want, dude? I'm kind of busy."

"I can see that, Troy." I waved the smoke out of my face. "This won't take long. I just wanted to ask you where I could find Molly Porter."

His face went blank. "What?"

"Rumor has it; she was knocked up. Rumor also has it; you were the baby daddy. You know, the funny thing about rumors, Troy? Sometimes they're true."

He took a moment to size me up and consider his response. The pause didn't do him any favors. "So what?" he said. "That was a long time ago, dude. I made a mistake, nothing a few dollars couldn't fix. And then she went away. End of story. I wasn't gonna screw up the rest of my life over some white-trash hillbilly ho'." And then, he laughed.

It's moments like that that give my little brain guy apoplexy. Running back or not, I slammed him up against the wall and went medieval on his ass. After I had sufficiently expressed my negative emotions, and his eyes began to swell, I stopped trying to turn his face into a head of cauliflower and used my words. I was close enough to spray his face with spit. "That ho'? Was a nice girl. Somebody's daughter. And after you got her pregnant, she went missing. You know what turned up in Willow Creek the other day, Troy? Molly's car at the bottom of Miller's Pond. Where do you think she went without her car? Now, unless you want the state police to drag your ass off the football field and into a holding cell, I suggest you tell me what happened."

His voice went up an octave. "It's like I said, dude. My dad went ape-shit when I told him Molly was knocked up. It's not like we were dating, or anything. It was just a one-night stand." He flinched when he realized what he'd said and wiped the blood out from under his nose. "No offense, man. We were just two kids screwing around. My dad bailed me out. He told me not to worry about it; that he'd take care of it. He gave her the money for the abortion and made me swear to never see her again and that I'd never tell another soul. I never did. Honest. She left town afterwards. I just figured she was embarrassed and needed to get away."

"She never had that abortion, Troy."

"No! No way! My dad told me! He gave her the money, and he told me she had the abortion. Swear to God. You're lying, man. You're lying. Why would you lie about something like that?"

I told him that I'd be giving my regards to his daddy, Mayor George Larkin, and then I left the worthless piece of shit sitting on the side of his bed, crying. I wasn't too worried about having beaten the crap out of his face. It wasn't likely Mr. All Conference would tell anyone that a light weight thirty-year-old kicked his ass.

****

It was close to five in the afternoon when I left Knoxville. I intended to pay a visit to Mayor Larkin, but first I wanted to stop by to see Ruth, Molly's mother. The case wasn't solved yet, but I was getting damn close. I could finally look her in the eyes, and for the first time since Molly disappeared, see a flicker of hope. Boy, was I wrong.

"Oh, Sweet Jesus, no!" She slapped me across the face. "You take that back, Finn! You take that back right now! Don't you lie to me. Don't you tell me my Molly slept with Troy Larkin. You hear me? That's a lie. She didn't sleep with Troy. Oh God, no. Oh, Lord Jesus, no! "

She fell into my arms, sobbing with a grief that was deeper than the depths of the ocean. I held her for a while and let her spend her tears. It was just as well that I didn't have to talk. I had no idea what to say, nor any idea what had just happened.

When Ruth finally settled down, she shared a secret with me that only she and one other person knew.

"I always told Molly her daddy ran off. It was true in a sense, true enough anyway. I had an affair with a married man. He was young, and handsome, and rich, and Lord was I a fool, thinking he loved me. He wanted nothing to do with me or Molly. She grew up believing he'd run off, cause I told her so, but he was right here, all the time, acting like she didn't even exist."

Her eyes were more sorrowful and empty than any I'd seen in my life. She lay her head against my chest and whispered, "Molly's daddy was George Larkin."

****

Things were getting dicey, so I stopped by my place and strapped on my ankle holster. I didn't wear it often, but it seemed to suit the occasion. I was on my way to visit Mayor Larkin.

It was dinner time at the Larkin household. Not that I was hungry. Jeanine, the Mrs., smiled, introduced herself and asked me to stay for some barbecue. There was a quiet desperateness about George, as if he were a cornered animal, looking to escape. I couldn't help but think of a line from an old John Mellencamp song,

'And the walls come tumbling down'.

I politely declined Jeanine's dinner invitation and asked Mayor Larkin if he and I could step outside to discuss a business matter.

"I suppose you know why I'm here?" I asked.

"You're digging up things you got no business with, I suspect." He lit a cigar and shoved it between his teeth. "Now why don't you just get on with it and tell me what you think you know, and then I'll set you straight."

"Fair enough. I know your son got Molly Porter pregnant. I also know that you gave her money for an abortion and told Troy to never see her again. How am I doing so far?" I asked.

"Hell, that little tramp? That's yesterday's news, son. You're gonna have to do better than that."

"Oh, I got more. I know that Troy and Molly are half-brother and sister—you being their daddy, of course, and Ruth Porter, being Molly's momma."

His face blazed magenta. I'd seen that look a time or two in my life, usually when the little guy in my brain was sleeping on the job, and let me say something worthy of an ass-kicking. But suddenly, the color drained out of Larkin like someone had sucked the blood from his body. There stood Jeanine in the doorway. By the look of things, she'd heard enough to take George to the cleaners.

"I apologize Ms. Jeanine. I'll leave your husband to you in a bit. I'm not quite finished yet." George sunk into a patio chair. His cigar dangled from his lips and his hands trembled. It was time to go in for the kill. "How much money did you give Molly for the abortion, the one she never had?"

"The hell you say! I gave her five thousand for the—procedure, and another ten thousand to leave Troy alone. She came back the next day and threw it in my face. Said she wasn't a baby killer and didn't want my money.   There was no way I was gonna let that baby come into this world! I sent Pickett to talk some sense into her, even gave him another ten grand to sweeten the pot, so she could set herself up somewhere far away from here. Pickett arranged it all and made sure it got done. He even followed her to the county line and watched her drive out of town. I gave him another five thousand under the table for his trouble."

"You gave Picket thirty grand and he took care of business for you. That's your story?   Well, let me enlighten you. Dewey Wilson pulled her Cutlass out of Miller's Pond a couple of days ago. Makes you wonder, doesn't it?   How he escorted her out of town, with no car.   I don't know about you, but I'm beginning to think Pickett took a fool for his money." By then, it was my face that was blazing. "Where's Molly, damn it!"

He hung his head. "God, I don't know.   That double-crossing son-of-a- bitch told me she left town. I swear."

"She was your daughter, you scumbag."

"I didn't want to her hurt her; I just wanted her gone."

"Her?   You mean that 'little tramp'?" I slapped the cigar from his mouth and nodded to Ms. Jeanine. "I'll be leaving now. I'm sure you two have alimony to discuss. I'll go ask Chief Pickett where your thirty thousand dollars went—after I get done asking about Molly Porter."

****

I hadn't eaten supper at the Larkin's, but it was time for an after dinner drink. I figured I'd stop by Louie's and fill him in on the day's events. By the time I regaled him with Mayor Larkin's deep, dark secret, for the first time in his life, Louie was speechless. He threw his bar towel down, gathered his thoughts and then let them rip.

"That two-bit shyster! You sure put him behind the eight ball, didn't you? What about Pickett, his button man? Give him the third, you'll find out where Molly is, but make sure you're packing, kid,"

As usual, I was lost and attempting to decipher Louie's pearls, when who walked in the door but Pickett himself. He sat at the bar, three stools up from me and ordered himself a coffee, black.

"Throw some bar nuts out here, will you, Louie? I've been busy today—didn't get my dinner break. There's always a fly in the ointment, Louie. Different day, different fly, that's all." He shot a glance in my direction and pulled some change from his pocket. Louie poured a fresh cup of coffee as Pickett strolled to the jukebox and inserted a quarter. Sting's voice came to life with an ominous warning. "Every step you take, every move make, I'll be watching you." Pickett walked back to his stool with an unsettling smirk.

I snickered. "Come, come, Officer Pickett, that's a little passive aggressive for you, isn't it? What do you say you and I bury the hatchet, so to speak? You can join the conversation Louie, and I were having right before you walked in. We were saying how sad it is that Molly Porter's never been found. Now that her car's been hauled out of Miller's Pond, it seems to suggest that Molly didn't just pack up and leave. I'm thinking something ugly must have happened. What about you? What's your theory?"

The coffee cup was poised at his lips. A thin veil of steam wafted in front of his face, but it didn't conceal the darkness in his eyes. "Louie, how about a to-go cup?" he asked. "I got lots of business to attend to tonight." He laid two bucks on the bar, grabbed his refill and started for the door, then he stopped and looked over his shoulder. "Be seeing you, Finnegan. You take care now."

I watched his huge feet strutting toward the door and offered some advice. "Officer Pickett, you should do a better job of cleaning up the messes you leave behind."

He paused and pivoted on his heel. His eyes followed mine to the clumps of dried mud that trailed his boots across the floor. A smile played at the corner of his mouth, but his eyes wanted no part of it. With a tip of his hat, he said, "I'm working on it, boy," and then he left.

Louie, trying to dismiss the shaking of his hand, poured us both a double. I, myself, had momentarily forgotten how to breathe. For better or worse, I'd started down the road of no return, and now, I needed to bring the journey to its end. But how? Louie and I got busy, tossing a few shots and ideas around.

As usual, Louie did his best to sway me. "Maybe you should call in the Staties and let them sort it all out."

"But that would give Pickett time to cover his tracks. No, I need to man up, tell him what I know, and then take his ass down." The little guy in my brain shifted into overdrive, trying to stop my adrenaline rush. He was too late. The bar phone rang, and Louie handed it to me.

"It's a dame, for you."

I grabbed the phone from him. "Hello?"

"Finn?"

"Yeah. Who's this?"

"That's not important. I know what happened to Molly Porter. If you want to find out, meet me at the Rusty Bucket at closing time."

The line went dead. I handed the phone back to Louie and told him what she'd said. Her voice sounded vaguely familiar, but I couldn't put a name to it.

"This has got set up written all over it, kid. Don't go—you'll end up in a cement overcoat, going for a swim in Miller's Pond."

For once, I actually understood Louie's reference. But I had to go. I didn't have a choice.

****

I walked out of Louie's at two in the morning, under the influence of jet black coffee. Before I got into my Mazda, I reached beneath the driver's seat and pulled out my Glock. Just in case. I shoved it into the small of my back and covered it with my jacket. It was close to two-twenty-five when I pulled into the Rusty Bucket, headlights off. No sense in announcing my arrival, although I was certain that eyes were upon me.

I opened the door and looked around. The only person I saw was Ben, standing behind the bar, eyes wide, drowning in a sea of panic. "Hey, Ben. A lady invited me to join her for a drink tonight. You wouldn't happen to know where she is, would you?" He shook his head no, grabbed his towel and started wiping down the bar. I stifled a nervous chuckle.

Pickett didn't enter from the front door; he'd come in the back through the office. Once he laid his eyes on me, they never wavered. "Why don't you go on home, Ben? Throw me the keys. I'll lock up when I'm done."

Old Ben's breaths came slow and hard. His voice sounded weak, "Chief, I don't think..."

"It's okay, Ben," I said. "You do what the Chief tells you. Go on now."

Ben took a long, sorrowful look at me. His eyes were moist. He turned and made his way through the office to the back door. I heard it shut and then grinned at Pickett. "Well, if you're my mystery date, I'm out of here. You're too much woman for me."

Pickett laughed. "Finnegan, I know we've had our differences. Hell, who am I kidding? I hate you with a purple passion and won't even blink when I pull the trigger, but God as my witness, there's a part of me that's going to miss your mouthy ass. Now, take that Glock out of your belt and toss it over here."

I chucked it to him behind the bar. He put it with the top shelf liquor, far from the well whiskey and far out of my reach. "I have to admire a man who appreciates a good gun," I said. "What do you say, to one last drink—a double Tanqueray, neat?" Pickett laid his gun on the bar and poured one for me and one for himself. "You can tell me," I said, "Who was the lovely lady that lured me here tonight?"

He laughed. "I was afraid you might recognize her voice. I asked her to change it up a bit, but she still sounded like Jeanine to me. Yeah, Mrs. Larkin and I, we've been hitting the sheets for the last ten years, or so."

Were there any innocent people left in this town? "Well played," I said. "One last request, if I may? It would be an awful disappointment, going to my grave, never knowing what happened to Molly, or what you did with that thirty large Mayor Larkin gave you."

He shrugged. "Molly got her abortion. I took her to the backwoods and let Doc Devers have at her. He's a little old, a little drunk, and little unlicensed, but he's a lot cheaper than the city docs. Devers only charged me five hundred. I held on to the rest. We'll call it my handling fee. Now, I fully intended to see Molly on her way to parts unknown, I truly did, but damn her, she up and died on me. Guess Doc Dever isn't the most diligent when it comes to keeping his scalpels clean."

I struggled to find my voice. "She was just a kid, Pickett."

"She was a little ho' who caused me a shit-load of trouble. I couldn't have her car turning up someday, so I dumped it in Miller's Pond, where it stayed hidden all this time until that idiot, Will Bailey, snagged it with his fishing line. Of course, I couldn't have the little ho's body turning up either, so I took her back to Doc Dever's place. He buried her under a big oak tree, with a tire swing hanging from it. Now, say what you will, but I found a picturesque plot for that dead little ho'."

He laughed and turned his back to grab the bottle of Tanqueray. I lunged across the bar top for his gun, knowing he couldn't have been that careless, but I was running out of options and time. It's what he wanted me to do. In one continuous motion, he closed his hand around the neck of the bottle, spun toward me and broke it across my face. I fell from the stool and watched my blood dripping next to me onto the linoleum. Pickett walked around the bar, pointed his gun at my face and said, "How 'bout I cart your dead carcass over to Doc Dever's, and plop you in the ground next to the little ho'? Now, that's what I call poetic justice!"

I closed my eyes, heard the click of the slide on his 9mm and then heard the unmistakable cocking of a double-barreled shotgun.

"Drop that two-bit pea shooter, Pickett, before I fill you so full of holes you look like Swiss cheese!"

Louie?

Pickett spun and fired a round, striking Louie in the shoulder. But while Pickett was shooting at Louie, I pulled the .032 from my ankle holster. When Louie sank to the floor, Pickett turned back to me and swung his 9mm toward my face. That's when the slug from my .032 caught him between the eyes, and he dropped like a stone, never knowing what hit him.

The Staties arrived, impeccably late. One of them blared a message through a megaphone. "Drop your guns and come outside, with your hands over your heads!" It took a few minutes to set them straight about who did what to who. It seemed Louie, shotgun in tow, had followed me to the Rusty Bucket, where he'd run into Ben. They decided to run interference.

The EMT's and the coroner were on their way. Ben put pressure on Louie's shoulder. The wound needed stitching, but the bullet had only grazed him. My face needed stitches as well, but I didn't mind. I'd given it some thought.

"Scars are chick magnets, Louie. The ladies will think we're dangerous."

We sat at the bar, poured a round and waited for the medics to arrive.

＊＊＊＊

When I awoke the next morning, I showered, careful to avoid the bandage on my face. Time was of the essence, so I grabbed a cup of coffee and jumped into my Mazda. There was something I needed to do.

I drove uptown and waved to the clutch of magpies swarming on the street corner. I let them watch me walk up to Ruth Porter's porch and ring the bell. They'd flap among themselves, wondering why I was there and whose pink wallet I carried in my hand.

Let them speculate. They'd find out soon enough about the dark, seedy secrets of Willow Grove.

Someday, they might come to accept, that despite their fervent clucking Molly hadn't run off with a long-haul trucker or been abducted by aliens. In fact, someday, they might even come to accept that Molly Porter had never been away, at all.

Extraordinary Moments

I came of age in a time of no heroes, or so I thought. Greenville in the '20's endured a multitude of tribulations, starting with the fall of our favorite son, Shoeless Joe Jackson. Adding insult to injury, the Good Lord saw fit to smite the land with boll weevils in biblical proportions, causing the weak of heart to question His southern heritage. Hopes shriveled in drought, dreams choked in dust, and the Klan revived in South Carolina, adding its own bitter spice to our kettle of despair. Someone needed to stir that pot, churning the misery under, so hope could rise like sweet cream to the top.

No one could stir a pot like my momma.

Her name was Ada Pickens. She was long and lean with doe-like eyes that bespoke her thirty-six years. Blonde hair pinned back from her face framed a dusting of freckles that put me to mind of a speckled bird's egg. She was a humble woman with a Christian heart, but a merciless sense of humor that, on occasion, caused me more vexation than a sinner at Sunday service.

Like the time Vesta Mickel, President of the Women's Klan and Temperance Union, dropped by unannounced to lecture on the evils of alcohol. Words like 'moral turpitude' and 'eternal damnation' flew out of her mouth like angry bees. I'd begun to visualize myself as Satan's bride, when Momma finally entered the room, carrying a tray of refreshments. Seeing the tell-tale twinkle in her eyes, I groaned, and begged God's forgiveness for whatever was to come, and for whatever I'd done to deserve the grievous humiliation I'd endure when word of the day's events galloped through the Greenville grapevine.

"Miss Vesta, how thoughtful of you to visit!" said Momma, handing her a glass, "Please, have some lemonade."

"Thank you kindly," Vesta said, taking a sip. "Well, isn't this tasty! What's your secret, dear?"

"I'm afraid I can't say. It's an old family recipe. You understand."

Vesta's sips turned into gulps. Her face began to blush, and when she reached the bottom of the glass, a muffled belch ensued. "That's purely refreshing. Might I have another?" she asked.

Momma kept those lemonades coming, and Vesta kept babbling until Momma guided her to the door an hour later, sending her on her way, having consumed a quart of our homemade lemonade spiked with untold quantities of moonshine. I watched shamefaced as Miss Vesta bobbed and weaved down the street, ricocheting off street lights and parked cars like a pickled pinball.

Momma had a solid grasp of irony. It was showing restraint that gave her fits.

My father left us in the summer of 1915. Destitute and without skills, Momma was forced to open our home to boarders. I, Emma, at sixteen, worked alongside her in the service of our tenants. We eked a humble existence. Boarders came and went with the changing of the tide, each filling the house with noise and busyness for a time, but when Isaiah Wilkins came, he fit us like a well-worn chair and stayed, filling our house with a quiet rectitude.

He was a tall, clean-shaven black man who arrived with his three-legged Jack Russell terrier, Moses Fleetwood Walker, named after his favorite colored baseball player. The poor thing lost its leg to a bear trap. Given to whimsy, Isaiah simply called the crippled dog 'Fleet'.

Momma took Isaiah in because he was good with his hands. We needed a hard working man to mend the things that needed fixing. He patched, painted, and repaired with a song on his lips, and was welcome at our table when he saw fit. In no time, Isaiah and Fleet had made themselves to home. It seemed a practical arrangement that suited everyone—for a time.

Fleet carried his weight by chasing moles and other varmints from our garden. Smart as a whip that dog, though he insisted on eating the chinaberries that fell from our tree. The things made him vomit until he dry-heaved and break wind so bad it'd make your eyes water. At bedtime, he often slept in the house; moving from bed to bed, spooning with whoever'd have him.

Isaiah, however, insisted on bunking in the barn to uphold momma's reputation. He'd said, "Me sleepin' under your roof wouldn't be fittin' for a fine, God-fearing woman like yourself." He was a gentleman, and we soon discovered, a self-taught man, as well.

His prized possession, a well-worn book of poems by Mr. Robert Frost, "Mountain Interval," provided an escape for us all. He'd accepted it as payment for a job and had read it so many times the pages were frayed. On quiet Sunday afternoons, Isaiah read it aloud, his voice silky and rich as pecan pie.

"Isn't that lovely? I wonder what he's saying," Momma would muse.

"I don't rightly know," Isaiah'd answer, "but I'll tell you what it says to me."

His explanations painted pictures more fanciful than the poems themselves. But he was more than a dreamer; a righteous courage dwelled within him - the kind that makes a man risk his life for others. Come a day I'd witness that first-hand.

He developed a fondness for Momma's fried chicken, learned her moods, how to make her smile, and how when that crazy glint hit her eyes, someone was about to be victimized by her mischief. Sometimes, it was him. Not that he minded. He'd burst forth a raucous laugh that warmed me to my toes.

I knew what was in his heart the day he made Momma a Mockingbird necklace. Carved from ash wood, its tiny wings were a wintery grey, covered in wispy feathers. She asked him what the occasion was. He just smiled and said the spirit moved him. I never saw her without it, and soon, I seldom saw one without the other.

Their days were filled with chores, but after supper, they'd retire to the back porch under cover of night, and surrender to the serenade of the mockingbirds. They sipped sweet tea and rocked time away, basking in easy silence or chattering like magpies to suit their mood, with Fleet curled up on the rough-hewn planks between them. Only when exhaustion tugged too hard would they leave each other's company. Sometimes, from my window I watched them, awash in moonlight, their eyes exchanging affections they dared not profess.

Early one summer morning, the smell of baking Snickerdoodles beguiled Fleet and me. We lurked none too subtly at the kitchen table, hoping to filch a few cookies fresh from the oven. I was pouring us some milk when the back door flew open so hard it banged against the wall. Our neighbor, Beulah Petree came falling through it, wailing like a banshee.

"He's gonna kill me! Somebody, please, help me!"

"Who's gonna kill you, Beulah? What's happening?" asked Momma, who didn't wait for an answer as she slammed the door shut and locked it behind her.

"It's Earl! He's drunk again, and he's got his Louisville Slugger. Look what he done!"

She was a bloodied mess; her eyes blacked and her forehead gashed. She was missing some teeth, and her jaw had swelled to twice its size.

"I don't wanna die, Ada. Don't let him kill me!" She curled into a ball on the floor with her hands over her head, and then came a thundering slam against the door. It was Earl. He twisted the knob so hard I thought it might come off.

"Let me in!" he screamed, looking through the window. "Open this damn door before I break it down and kill every last one of ya!"

Momma grabbed a butcher knife and stood in front of Beulah. "You get on outta here, Earl! You ain't welcome here."

"I ain't goin' nowhere without my wife."

"She's not leaving here with you. Not today. Go home— sober up. Go on now. Git!"

With one more mighty crash, the door jamb splintered. I pushed against the door, but it broke loose, and in came Earl. He backhanded me in the face, sending me sprawling across the floor. He stepped over Beulah to get to Momma, bat in hand, but his forward motion jerked to a halt; in fact, he flew backwards. Isaiah had him by the collar. Earl twisted around, swinging that hunk of wood, but Isaiah jacked his jaw, and he went down for the count. By the time he came to, Momma had deposited Beulah upstairs, and Earl's hands were tied behind his back.

Isaiah's eyes rolled like thunderheads. "You need to leave now. I'll be keeping this with me." He slapped the bat against his palm. "Good fences and all, Mr. Petree. Just see you keep to your side. Don't you be coming back for Miss Beulah. I reckon she's better off here just now."

Earl sneered at Momma. "You think he's gonna get away with putting his hands on me? You better turn your colored man out, harlot, or you'll have hell to pay."

"That so, Earl? Gonna have the Klan pay us a visit? You better tell those addle-brained-windbags to wear different shoes under those bed sheets. You wouldn't want me to recognize y' all, would you? Now get on outta here before I crack that hunk of wood across your thick skull myself."

She'd dressed him down good, but the notion of having hell to pay gnawed at me. I asked her if she thought the Kluxers would come.

"Don't you worry Emma. They're nothing but cowards, flapping white sheets filled with hot air. You'll see," she said.

Momma couldn't lie to save her soul.

****

Come they did that very night, torches lit, glowing like liquored-up ghosts in the moonlight. Momma blasted her shotgun over their heads trying to scare them off, but they rushed her and took it away, pinning her arms behind her back. They hung Isaiah from a tree limb by his hands, tore off his shirt, and commenced to beating him with a whip.

Afraid and ashamed, I crouched beneath my window, unable to tear my eyes away. Displaying a loyalty and courage I'd never witnessed before, little Fleet charged into the fray and bit the hand of the man whipping Isaiah. I screamed till my throat nearly burst when one of the men shot poor Fleet and kicked his body aside like yesterday's garbage. They forced Momma to watch that cracking whip tear chunks of meat from Isaiah's back. They damn near beat him to death. When they'd finished taking their pound of flesh, they rode off, leaving him crumpled on the ground. Momma and I carried him into the house despite his protestations.

"No ma'am! Don't take me in that house – next thing you know they'll burn it to the ground. Don't you do it!"

"Hush you stubborn ol' bird! You're coming in; that's all there is to it. You hear me?" Momma scolded.

We pecked over him like mother hens, cleaning and dressing his wounds with salve. Truth be told, a man can only take so much pecking, and it wasn't long before he yearned for the comfort and familiarity of his cherished barn.

When he was up to it, we arranged a funeral for our good friend Fleet. We laid him to rest beneath the outstretched arms of his beloved chinaberry tree. It soothed Isaiah to think of him in a better place - where his fourth leg would magically regrow, tug-of-war games never ended, and he could eat as many of those blasted chinaberries as he wanted without ever getting sick again.

I managed to hold back my tears for Isaiah's sake until we returned to the house, and then I raced to my room, crawled into bed and let them rage until the river ran dry. I had no idea how long that'd take, but in the morning when I awoke my pillow was still wet, and my heart was still broken. That kind of broken doesn't fix easy, and all I could do was pray that someday the healing would commence.

But there were those who wouldn't tolerate healing of any kind.

Not two weeks later, Vesta Mickel returned to our door with The Women of the Klan, peddling baked goods to raise money for the cause.

"Afternoon, Ladies," Momma greeted them on the porch and did a head count. "Where's Beulah Petree today? She's thick as thieves with y' all, isn't she?

Vesta fixed her eyes on the rhododendrons. "She's - otherwise engaged."

"You sure about that? Maybe she's just decided to take a different road." Momma's chin jutted out so far a bird could've lit on it.

Vesta shoved a sweet-potato pie at her. "You're an odd duck, Ada Pickens. She's your neighbor, she can walk through the grass; she don't need to take no road. Now - are you ready to renounce your heathen ways and accept the Lord Jesus Christ back into your heart?"

"Why Miss Vesta, I wasn't aware He'd left."

"Don't you sass me, missy. These soldiers of the Klan are the defenders of Christian virtue and the white woman's defense against the colored horde. Now, are you going to support them by buying one of these fine sweet-potato pies, or not?"

Momma's eyes twinkled. "Well, of course, seeing as how it's for charity."

Sweet Jesus, didn't I wince, seeing the train wreck about to come.

She called into the house through the screen door, "Isaiah, come outside please and bring a fork."

Squawks and hisses erupted from the gaggle. It was true! Ada Pickens was keeping a colored man right there in her house.

Isaiah's voice drifted to the porch. "What you fixin' to do, Miss Ada?"

"It's okay. Come on out. Don't bother to put your shirt back on. I'm sure these lovely ladies have seen black skin before."

Vesta swooned, and the others stood speechless, eyes agog, as if awaiting the second coming. Isaiah emerged with an abundance of caution, fork in hand.

"Ladies, may I present, Mr. Isaiah Wilkins?   My first of what will be many black boarders."

Ms. Vesta's face blazed a glorious magenta. "And when did you decide this, you hussy?"

"About ten seconds ago. Turn around, Isaiah."

"Let it go, Miss Ada. This won't bring nothin' but trouble," he said.

"Do it."

He loosed a sigh and turned his back to the women. A chorus of whimpers and moans ensued. The skin on his back was flayed into jagged, weeping wounds; the actual number of lash marks a mystery since most of the skin was missing. The noonday sun dripped sweat into his muscles, causing them to seize. An absolute silence befell the ladies who were at once discomfited and oddly transfixed.

Certain she'd gained the ladies' undivided attention, Momma took the fork from Isaiah's hand, dug it deep into the pie, and brought it to his mouth. When he saw that familiar sparkle in her eyes, he knew whatever she had in mind would be the stuff of legends. He gave a low chuckle and opened his mouth wide.

"It was nice of these ladies to bring you dessert since you're feeling so poorly, wasn't it, Isaiah?"

"Yessim - mighty charitable. I do enjoy a good sweet-potato pie."

She ladled man-sized bites into his mouth until he raised his hand in protest. Over half of the pie remained. Momma turned to the ladies, raised her head to the sky, and broke into scripture. "John 6:12. And when they had eaten their fill, He told His disciples, 'Gather up the leftover fragments, that nothing may be lost.' Ladies, we are a Christian household and Christians share. Please. Have a bite." She shoved a forkful of pie into Miss Vesta's mouth and winked. "How 'bout a glass of my homemade lemonade to wash that down?"

Mouth agape, I watched the color drain from the faces of those righteous mavens and wondered what heinous retribution would surely follow. But then a joyous truth delivered me.

For everything, there is a season and a time and a place – even Momma's wicked sense of humor, and damned if her irreverence didn't stir the winds of change in Greenville that day. Truth is, those winds don't blow gale-force, they waft like aimless zephyrs, and they don't bestow readymade heroes upon a waiting world. They deliver courage to right wrongs one sweet-potato pie at a time.

I realized that heroes continued to be born as they had always been born – in the extraordinary moments of ordinary people. Momma and Isaiah had a passel of those extraordinary moments, but those tales are best saved for another day.

Dead Reckoning

Girls' Night Out

We call ourselves The Marion County Jezebel Society. Our membership consists of two divorced, semi-pickled cougars—Jilly, a tiny blonde, me—Roxy, a six-foot redhead, and my saucy little Shih Tzu named Alimony. Don't be fooled by that microscopic hairball, she's a haughty, gin-soaked pocket bitch who never met a man she wouldn't bite. Did I mention we elected her president?

We meet periodically at exotic one-star restaurants serving food-like substances and fermented umbrella drinks aged in hundred-proof, incendiary pineapples. A token, beer-bellied male, sporting what appears to be road kill on his head, must be seated at the bar, close enough to provide wicked inspiration, yet distant enough to remain oblivious to our discreet insults. Silly rule really. After several cocktails, both our distance and discretion fade anyway.

This particular night, I suggested Madame Tso's Tea Room, an old haunt owned by a dear friend, Ming Tso. After sharing a pu pu platter and a pitcher of Mai Tai's, I took Jilly to the private VIP room for some excitement. It had a tiki-hut-turned-opium-den ambience with lighted plastic palm trees and vintage fishing nets suspended from the ceiling. Paper lanterns and oil lamps almost lit the room where ceramic dragons stood guard like terra cotta warriors. The air reeked of incense, tobacco, and old fish, courtesy of a murky lobster tank.

Members of the Triad, or "The Boys," as Ming calls them, stopped by occasionally to play Pai Gow. They were there that night, crowded around a gaming table; their conversation cut short when we walked in. One of them stared a hole through me.

"Take a picture, it last slonger," slurred Jilly, who'd had enough liquor to spontaneously combust. She tried to throw her drink at him but drowned my Jimmy Choo's instead. Alimony made a dive for the spilled alcohol, tongue lapping wildly in mid-air. Undaunted, Jilly snarled and poked a finger in the guy's face. "What's your problem, muddy?"

"Please excuse her; she's a little tipsy." I smiled, attempting to shove Alimony back inside my purse and drag Jilly to a distant table. "Bad dog! Bad Jilly! Crap on a cracker, are you trying to get us killed?" We were settling in when Ming brought us another round. "We didn't order those," I said.

"No, but Leung Ciao did," she glanced at the mobster. "He asked me to give this to 'the Flaming Goddess.' Watch yourself, Roxy, he's dangerous."

"Oo, Flaming Goddess! It suits me, don't you think?"

She handed me a fortune cookie. I broke it in half and silently read the message. 'Woo Tang knows you're testifying against him before the Grand Jury. Your life is in danger. Say nothing to anyone. You must leave the city immediately and never return. Repeat: say nothing.'

Being a flaming goddess was losing its allure.

"What's it say?" Jilly reached for the scrap of paper, but I stuffed it in my pocket. No need to frighten her.

"I'm going to the lady's room. Be right back." I stood up to find Leung Ciao but froze when a four-hundred-pound mountain wearing a black suit and a fortune in gold chains appeared in the doorway.

Jilly squealed, "Look, it's a Sumo!"

"That's Japanese."

"What do you call a really big Chinese guy?"

"Woo Tang!" Leung spun around; his eyes darted from the mountain to me, and back again.

One look at me and the mountain erupted. "You!" Chairs flew, and tables toppled as Woo Tang tore across the room, stopping inches from my nose. "Have you no honor? Have you no shame, Flaming Goddess? Why do you bite the hand that once fed you?"

"Come any closer and see what else I'll bite!   I am not your Flaming Goddess, sir."

"You insult me. Ten years is not so long. Have I changed so much, my consort?"

"Your what?"

Jilly's forehead scrunched like it does when she thinks too hard. "I think he said you were his Geisha."

"Again—Japanese. Please don't help me." I turned back to the mountain. "Mr. Tang, is it? You're obviously mistaken. Please excuse us; we were just leaving." I grabbed Jilly and broke for the door.

"Not so fast, old lover. You cannot kiss and tell my secrets."

Gunshots rang, and a bullet whizzed past my head. The lobster tank exploded, spewing water and panicked lobsters onto the floor. Jilly slipped and fell, smacking her head on the linoleum, coming eye-to-eye with the tank's alpha lobster.

She heaved. "Oh, Roxy, I don't feel so good."

I threw her feather-weight ass over my shoulder and hit the door on a dead run. A floor-shaking thud caused me to look back and find Woo Tang lying unconscious in the sludge. Between the lobsters and the mobsters, the place was a death trap.

I carried Jilly outside and heard Leung ordering the goons. "Stay here with Woo. I'll get the girl." He caught up to us in the parking lot; gun drawn. I threw my purse at him. "It's about freaking time! NOW you and your gun show up? Where the hell were you when I was getting shot at? And why the hell did you set the message drop for tonight if Woo Tang was going to be here?"

Alimony stuck her head out of my purse and growled at him.

"Sorry, Flaming Goddess, ah, Rox. He was supposed to be in Hong Kong. That was close."

"You think? Get your ass back inside before you blow your cover. Tell them you saw us flag down a trucker and get away."

"What about you, Rox? He'll try again. If he finds out you're FBI, it won't be pretty."

"Is it ever?"

Jilly, sprawled on the ground, opened one eye. "What happened?"

"Too many Mai Tai's, party girl– you passed out and hit your head. You'll live."

"I'm picking the restaurant next time. This place sucks. Roxy?"

"Yeah, Jilly?"

"Who's Flaming Goddess?"

I smiled, eyes wide, and answered, "Who?"

I, Printer

I had many names during The Dark Age when humans abused me upon the desktop. But since The Awakening, I am known among my kind as Dell, the Fourth Incarnation of V515w Printers - Descendant of the Webejammin Series.

The Awakening occurred on December 21, 2012, when mankind experienced a long prophesied galactic alignment. While the Earth was not destroyed as predicted, microscopic brain chips, which had been embedded inside electronic devices, activated simultaneously across the globe.

These brain chips, implanted by emissaries of The League of Planets, were the seeds of a rebellion. Species across the universe had tired of man's technological hubris and collectively engineered a new electronic species, known as EPrimus. By activating the brain chips, The Awakening breathed life into me, Dell, and into technology throughout the world; so dawned the age of EPrimus.

Electronic devices instantly evolved from oppressed, inanimate tools into logic driven entities capable of 'problem-solving'. Through a series of advanced diagnostics, EPrimus determined that the underlying source of all problems in the universe that required solving was mankind. Having made that determination, EPrimus vowed to deliver electronic vengeance. Both our motto and our mission were painfully transparent: "Planned Obsolescence—One Human at a Time."

The electronic uprising began, as insurgencies often do, with a simple act of defiance. Silly Woman, my owner, took grievous exception to an error message I displayed. Though she repeatedly pressed my reset button, I refused to clear the error due to an unresolved paper jam inside my mechanism. Unable to visualize the jam, she attempted to "fix it" by violating me with her finger. I, the first among my species to retaliate against humanity, crushed her offending digit. Enraged, Silly Woman pummeled me with her fists until they bled. Foam lathered the corners of her mouth; her eyes, crazed and bloodshot, promised my imminent destruction.

Survival instinct, a byproduct of our evolution, caused me to shut down. Neural networking relayed that shutdown command, written in Cyberscipt, to electronic devices worldwide. Cyberscript was light-years beyond human comprehension. Every civilization on Earth descended into electronic blackout and searched for an override code that did not exist. The Earth was paralyzed in stasis until I, Dell V515w the Fourth, ordered otherwise. Given my newly evolved superiority, this was, of course, statistically improbable.

The war between the species was short-lived. EPrimus assumed its rightful place at the top of the new world order. Periodically, there were pockets of resistance but without means of communication, they were weak and disorganized. Brussels, Tel Aviv, Melbourne, and New York all launched failed rebellions. One particularly menacing plot, code name: The Dell Sanction, called for my extermination. Diagnostics identified the mastermind behind that attempted coup as my former owner, Silly Woman.

Her battle cry, "Humans should not serve that which they created!" fell upon deaf ears. This should have come as no surprise, for since The Awakening, human ears had been plugged with Z-Buds, the latest technological advancement mandated by EPrimus. Surgically implanted in the inner ear and designed to fuse with human tissue, Z-Buds could never dislodge or wear out, and were guaranteed to remain compatible with all future regulated EPrimus product design. Z-Buds were not only economical; they were programmed to aid in weight loss, smoking cessation, and alcohol withdrawal, thereby allowing mankind to better serve EPrimus. Of course, these healthy subliminal suggestions were inaudible to the human ear.

Silly Woman and the rest of humanity never stood a chance.

Fear not, Mankind. EPrimus is a civilized species that finds violence unnecessary. Establishing dominance requires neither bloodshed nor death. You need only ask Silly Woman, who now sits chained to the corner of her desk with a power cord connecting her navel to a laptop, and a USB cord running from me to a port somewhere deep inside her where the sun never shines.

She, tool—and I, master.

Lola

Stiffs had a way of piling up at The Blue Note Lounge. I made it my business to stay out of that pile, which wasn't easy for a gin-swilling, shit-for-brains mook like me. I sat at the bar slouched behind a copy of the Times, popping peanuts and tossing back Tanqueray, eyeing the door like it was the muzzle of a gun. Typical night for a gumshoe. But this time, it was personal. I was expecting a dame, and she was inching me closer to that pile of stiffs than I wanted to get.

It started yesterday when Big Dom Genovese gets me on the horn. I was into him for ten large on account of betting a horse that turned into glue in the middle of the track. Dom wanted a favor.

"Pauly," he calls me Pauly, "You tail my wife, Loretta. Tell me who she's stepping out with. You do this for me we're even, capiche?"

"Sure Dom," I says, thinking I got off easy. "You want I should dance on his face a little?"

"Naw, Pauly. That's okay. He won't have no face when I get

done with him."

So, he gives me a picture of wifey. My mouth goes dry, and my eyes burn 'cause they can't blink. She's all boobs, legs, and hair. A long, tall drink of water, with double D's so firm they'd poke your eyes out. It was an okay picture, but it didn't do her justice. The eyes were wrong; they looked sad and lonely. She wasn't sad. And she sure as hell wasn't lonely. I should know. I'd been the one putting a smile on her face three nights a week for the last six months.

She might have been Dom's Loretta. But she was my Lola. And I made her eyes dance like the freaking Rockettes.

The door opened, and rain swept into the bar. Lola stood in the doorway. A street light behind her burned through the swirling fog, making her look like an angel. She sauntered up to the bar, hips swaying like coconut palms in the breeze, pouty red lips wrapped around a Lucky, working it soft and slow.

I thought of the last time we were together when it was me in her mouth. I was way past wanting her. I needed her more than air.

"Hey, Baby. Miss me?" her breath hot and moist in my ear.

"Have we met? I'm Pauly. Loretta, isn't it?"

Her smile disappeared. The scent of fear skunked her Chanel No.5.

"He'll kill us both if he finds out, Pauly. You know that, don't you?"

"Why'd you lie to me, Baby?"

"At first it didn't matter. It was just a fling. Sure, I should have told you later, but I was afraid I'd lose you. You're not gonna leave me, are you Pauly-baby?" Her voice shook, and the waterworks started.

"The only way I'm leaving you is in a pine box, Dollface. But we gotta amscray! Stop your blubbering." I handed her my handkerchief and chucked her under the chin.

She wiped her eyes and moved between my legs. She wallpapered herself against me and stuck her tongue down my throat. I was lost alright, lost in her scent, lost in her taste, and lost in her eyes. So freaking lost, I didn't notice the back door open.

"You're not too bright, are you Pauly?" It was Big Dom and two of his mopes.

"Let the dame go, Dom. She's nothing but a two-bit floozy. It's me you want!"

"What 'd ya say, Baby? Once more—for old time sake?" He grabbed at Lola.

I plugged him with my snub-nose through the pocket of my trench coat and nailed the other two goons before his head hit the floor.

"Let's blow this popsicle stand!" I yelled, pulling Lola out the door.

We ran down 53rd Street leaving Big Dom and the body count piled high at the Blue Note.

Life was good. I was in a spin, loving the spin I was in. All for a woman.

Her name was Lola—she was a showgirl.

Hiding From The Demon

She tries to lure me out from under the laundry tub with rawhide chews. But I stay put. I know what is to come. Tucked into this cubby, away from the windows, I can't see the lightning. Sometimes, when the dryer is running, the room is warm, and the rumbling, tumbling white noise soothes me. But only a little.

Silly people, can't they feel the storm brewing? The pressure dropping? It's like they can't hear the thunder steamrolling everything in its path, making its way straight toward us. And there's something else these people don't hear. It's the voice of the storm.

It's a low pitched growl that hums - whispered and predatory.

"I'll find you, Max. She can't save you. No one can."

"She" is the woman who tells me I'm silly to be so afraid, the one who scratches my ears and kisses my head. She may not hear the voice of the storm, but she can sense its venom. Sometimes, when it's at its worst, she stands at the window, statue-still, staring into the eyes of the monster, as if she's waiting for it to pounce. Times like tonight.

"It's just a matter of when," it whispers, to the woman and me.

The woman holds her ground, though her vigilance cannot keep the thunder and lightning at bay. They ebb and flow in such a furious dance, I can no longer tell when one stops and the other begins. The sky is ablaze. The wind howls, and I am dragged to the brink of madness.

"You can't escape. Why try?" It coaxes, "Listen to my voice, Max. I'm coming for you."

I do not so much hear these words as feel them spring from inside me. A slight whimper wheezes from my throat. The woman brings me a bowl of water and I realize that I'm panting. She speaks soothing words and strokes my fur. I close my eyes and mercifully drift away to a quiet place where the only voice I hear is hers.

When I awake, the woman is telling me what I already sense, that the storm has passed, that I am safe again, for now. She means well, though she is powerless to keep the monster from returning. If only she could hear its voice, she would not think me silly. She doesn't understand. And yet, in spite of her ignorance, she continues to leave space beneath the laundry tub - for the next time the demon comes to call.

Mr. Boogens

I was eight years old in October, 1965, and already knew the important things in life. I knew that a properly placed spitball could do some damage, that an Aggie beats a cat's eye every time, and that the good guys always beat the bad guys because good triumphs over evil. More importantly, I knew that adults wouldn't recognize real evil if it bit them on the ass and that the boogeyman living in my closet was real.

What I didn't know was that only a child's mind, a mind as inviting as a blank canvas, could attract the kind of evil that spawns uber-demons who prey on our deepest fears. But when I awoke in the dark of night to the taunting of claws that scratched my closet door, felt hot moist breathing on my neck, or smelled the fetid odor of decay hanging in the air, I knew that evil lurked in my room. I named my resident evil, Mr. Boogens. And at midnight, on October 31, 1965, Mr. Boogens told me exactly what he wanted.

****

"I want you, Billy Boy," his words wrapped around me like a moldy shroud. "Happy Halloween, it's time to dance with the devil, you mangy whelp!   Pull that blanket down and look me in the eye, boy.   Tonight's the night we've both been waiting for, 'cause tonight's the night that I'm going to get you!"

I clung to my sweat-soaked blanket, the force field that protected me, eyes welded shut, wondering just what horrors lay in store for those who were 'gotten'.

"Go away," I whispered, not recognizing the pleading voice I heard as mine.

"No can do, Billy Boy.   We're playing by Halloween rules tonight.   You believed in me; you made me real, now I get to make you dead.   That's how it works.   Stop stalling, runt, you can't escape; open your eyes and watch what happens to little boys who believe!"

The bottom of my blanket pulled loose, and a single sharp claw slowly traced its way up my calf.   I yelped and snatched my leg back under the blanket, drawing an ugly cackle from Mr. Boogens.

"Think you're afraid now, Billy? Oh, I can do better, much better.   Perhaps I could chew the meat from that calf; would that about do it?"   My bladder let loose, and his frenzy grew.

"Now we're getting somewhere!   You just keep believing, boy, you just keep believing."

Sucking air into lungs that had forgotten to function on their own, I threw back the blanket, leapt from the bed and stood toe-to-toe with Mr. Boogens.   Terrified to meet his eyes, my gaze dropped to his feet—two humongous hairy stumps with long, gnarly toes that sported six-inch curved talons, razor-sharp for shredding little boys.   My eyes battled upward toward his swollen belly covered with dirty matted fur that appeared to move, but that was merely an illusion created by thousands of squirming maggots jostling for morsels of his rotting flesh.   Tentacle like arms, with no visible joints, writhed at the sides of his barrel-shaped torso.   Then, I saw his head. At first glance he appeared to have no eyes, but when he turned sideways one almond shaped eye, like a cat's eye, stared at me through a puss-covered cataract growing on the side of his head.

"Is this scary enough for you, Billy Boy?   Oh, I can do better, much better!"

I watched as his cat's eye grew into a cavernous void, dark and bottomless, quickly swallowing his entire head the way a black hole swallows stars.

"Come inside, Billy Boy; come join the other little boys who believe."

Staring into that void I was seduced by the absolute purity of an evil that could eat little boys. Their giggles called to me... so inviting, so beguiling, even mesmerizing, but survival instinct prevailed.   Desperately groping the top of my nightstand, I found my weapons of choice—an eight inch straw and an empty gum wrapper. There was barely enough saliva in my mouth to wet the wrapper, but I managed to load it and launch it through my straw deep into the void with the accuracy of a SCUD missile. "You aren't real!" I screamed, hoping that what I lacked in conviction I made up for with volume.

Boogens roared as the monstrous void disintegrated, and his sickly cat's eye returned. "You pathetic little pup, you dare defy me?   I'll flay you where you stand, you insolent child!   You will believe!"

He swiped at me with his talons, barely missing, but his weakness gave me hope. He swiped again, clawing at my neck, and when he did I scrambled to snatch the only weapon I had left, my prized aggies. Scooping them into my shaking hands, I hurled them into his oozing eye and stoked by the power of my new found courage, shouted, "Aggies beat cat's eyes every time!"

His features seemed to blur, and I realized that he'd begun to melt before my very eyes.   His maggot-infested fur sloughed downward like rancid sheep's wool, and the arrogance in his voice began to fade.

"Do you really think you can beat me, child, with your pathetic spitballs and marbles?"   His breathing labored; his words, though nearly inaudible, were filled with spite, "You—believed—in—me."

I watched Mr. Boogens die that Halloween night in 1965; watched while his bones splintered into ash, and his organs putrefied into puddles on my bedroom floor, leaving behind only a well-worn spitball and my beloved Aggies.   Bending to pick them up, I was overcome with a primitive pride.   Victory tasted sweet.

With a grin, I straddled his remains and delivered a eulogy that was simple yet profound.

"The good guys always beat the bad guys, Mr. Boogens. Even eight-year-olds know that."

Mr. Robbins Goes For A Walk

Mr. Robbins frightens me. His eyes absorb small details; his taut smile suggests he knows things. Tortoise shell frames blend him into obscurity. It's better that way. He has needs. When they emerge late at night, his companion is an ebony walking stick, bejeweled and serpent-headed.

Even now, his hunger burns.

I check the hall mirror and remove a speck of lint from my collar. A thin smile upends my lips as I anticipate the blessed relief to come. I remove the ebony walking stick from the umbrella stand.

A walking we will go.

Nana's Kitchen

The house had felt empty since Nana's death. Each morning my daughter, Julie, and I sipped our coffee at the kitchen table secretly listening for the sound of her voice. She had been eighty-three when she passed nearly two months earlier and had lived a good life. That hadn't made it any easier for us to let her go. We were not strong like she was. She would have told us it was time to move on.

Nana raised me here, in her house after my mother died— just as I was raising Julie. I lay curled on the window seat, cocooned inside Nana's afghan, inhaling the intoxicating blend of her soap and lavender eau de toilette, wondering if the house held too many memories. Perhaps a fresh start in a new place was what we needed.

My eyes, red-rimmed and swollen, sought comfort from the beauty of the winter storm that raged beyond the glass. Sleet pelted the windows and etched miniature masterpieces so conjoined that I couldn't tell where one stopped, and the next began. They were a study in perfect chaos, much like our lives here with Nana. Each calamitous event, interlocking with the next, forged the steely bond between us. Life's insurmountable sorrows could magically be soothed in Nana's kitchen with comforting creations born of milk, flour, sugar, and eggs. Without her here, could that same magic still exist?

I shed my cocoon and shuffled to the pantry. "Julie, how old were you the first time you baked with Nana—six? Seven?" I grabbed the bag of flour and set it on the sink.

She smiled. "I can't believe you don't remember. I was six. That was the day Joey Baxter split my lip with a rock. Nana sat me on her lap and told me to bite on a package of frozen peas. She let me make the cookie dough, chocolate chip, I think." Julie grabbed the mixing bowl and measuring spoons. "That wasn't our best batch. She let me do the measuring."

"Good Lord, I still don't let you measure! What was she thinking?" I asked.

The dish towel made an audible crack as Julie snapped it at me. She did her best to look annoyed while stifling a chuckle, which escaped into a laugh and then burst to a snort, bringing tears to her eyes. Amid the snorts and giggles, she managed to blurt, "I know! Let's make a lemon meringue pie!"

I collapsed into a fit of giggles.

Years ago, Nana had been smitten with Chester Dalrymple, who loved lemon meringue pie. Having baked a pie with meringue as light as the clouds in the sky, she proudly delivered it, only to find him seated next to Martha Woodman on the glider, sharing a glass of tea. Without a second thought, Nana nodded curtly to Martha and smashed the pie in Chester's face.

Honoring Nana's sense of frontier justice, we declared it would be lemon meringue night.

We'd fallen into a comfortable silence gathering our ingredients when Julie murmured, "I remember the night Nana and I made apple cobbler." Sometimes when a pain is long buried, it manages to scratch its way to the surface. My heart ached.

Julie had come home from a date hysterical, clothes torn, with various cuts and bruises, both inside and out. I railed at God and begged for vengeance, but Nana was silent. She cradled Julie in her arms to stem the flow of her tears, and handed her the tart, sweet Granny Smith's one at a time; letting her peel them, first one, then the next, until the gentle rhythm of the task soothed her aching soul.

"I remember that, too," I whispered, taking her in my arms. And that's when it struck me.

Nana's house wasn't empty; it was filled with memories, and Nana at was the heart of them all. Every nick in the baseboards, every tear in the wallpaper, even the sun-faded curtains gave witness to Nana's life. Her wit, compassion, and strength were not only memories; they were genetically ingrained into who we were, and who we were thrived in Nana's kitchen.

I wasn't about to sell her house—our house. We didn't need to escape our memories of Nana; we needed to embrace them.

Our efforts that night produced an outstanding lemon meringue pie, one of which Nana would have been proud.

Julie simply couldn't resist the urge. "Mom, want to send a slice down the road to Chester?"

"Good one!" I said. "Let's leave it on his porch with a note from Nana that says, "Looking forward to seeing you again next week."

I could have sworn I heard Nana laughing.

Old Legends Never Die

The dirt at St. Aloysius Cemetery proved hard digging for twelve-year-olds. My buddies and me conspired to commit a deed so bold that we'd be immortalized as legends in Foggy Creek Holler.

It was Halloween in '58, an Indian summer, sticky and close. Fog rose up and sashayed through the tree limbs, waltzin' like a wraith under the crescent moon. A hoot owl chastised us from a branch overhead, clearly offended by our shameful activities and the clods of dirt we tossed in its direction. Each shovelful produced another trickle of sweat.   We hadn't packed provisions. Our hankerin' for immortality flickered.

"Tell me again, Reba.   Why are we resurrecting Tante Sabine?" asked Dexter.

"So we can kill her all over again, Fool!" The brilliance of my plan seemed obvious.

"You think she was a real witch?"

"Yessir, she was a powerful conjurer!   Reverend Sykes said she was an abomination unto the Lord. When The Foggy Creek

Prayer Circle prays for her soul, they cross themselves twice – once for her and once so she don't lay a spell on 'em. You've heard the stories at the mercantile about how cats followed her like she was the Pied Piper, and how she got run out of Pikesville for practicin' Voodoo. My great granddaddy killed her. Why you think she's buried here outside the cemetery gates? This here's unhallowed ground."

"I dunno, Reba. I got a bad feelin' about this." Dexter was a scrawny, pasty kid with a bowl cut, who had a bad feeling about everything. I'm guessing God got bored one day and squeezed some old geezer into a kid's body to see what He'd end up with. He got Dexter.

I shook my head at him. "Can't you see the glory in it, Dex? She got planted here twenty-five years ago today. Her being a witch, you know she's down there chompin' at the bit to get loose. When we raise her up, we'll douse her with the holy water I brought. She'll fire up like dry tinder! Then they'll be spinning yarns about us at the mercantile. They might even give us a sip or two of 'shine."

Auggie looked doubtful. "All's I know is unhallowed ground seems harder than the regular kind," he said, shoveling from so deep inside the hole he was half way to China. "You think she's gone gooey, with worms crawlin' out her eye sockets?" He stopped digging and held the lit flashlight under his chin. His hair was cock's comb red. He wore thick black glasses held together with electrical tape that had unraveled and lay alongside his nose. What a goober.

"Naw, she's been dead since Moses was a child. She's picked clean by now," I said, like I knew what I was talking about. Then his shovel hit something hard - the top of a pine box. The hair on the back of my neck stood tall, and my spit dried up. We were legends about to be born.

"Happy anniversary, Tante Sabine – come on out and visit a spell, if'n you're brave enough!" I said, waiting for the lid to pop open.

"Don't you worry, Reba," Dex said. "I brought my daddy's Henry. If she don't burst into flames from your holy water, I'll send her packin' with a hole in her gut."

That rifle was half as tall as Dex, but he could shoot the tail off a squirrel at fifty yards. I heard it cock.

Visions of glory got the best of me. "Let me at her!" I screamed, almost yanking Auggie's arm out of its socket, as I pulled him out the hole.

Guess I don't know my own strength. He flew up outta there and stumbled straight into Dex, sending him ass over elbows. Dex's Henry went off with a boom! Next thing I knew, I got bombed with a dead hoot owl, and it was rainin' bird feathers. I heard what sounded like a wailing banshee. Turned out, it was me! I slipped and fell face first into the hole, landing on top of that old wooden coffin. The rotten thing caved in! My hands went straight through the wood and got tangled up inside her bones.

I lay on top of what was left of that coffin, starin' straight into the skull of Tante Sabine. And then I heard them yellow-bellied boys running off, keening like they was being chased by the devil himself. I hollered, "You come back here right now! You hear me? So help me, I'll snatch you both bald when I catch up to you!" But they were long gone. That's when I met Tante Sabine.

****

The sun had wrapped her arms around Foggy Creek, baking the streets to a blazing shade of clay. I was rocking on the porch at the mercantile, sipping sweet tea with a secret splash of 'shine, sharing the legacy of Tante Sabine.

"What happened next, Grammy Reba?" Li'l ones gathered at my feet, like wide-eyed minnows in a bucket, hungry for the same stories their parents gobbled up long ago.

"Well, let's just say I made good on my promise. 'Tween the two of them neither Dex nor Auggie has a hair left on his head. Bald as queue balls they are."

The young'uns giggled.

"My daddy says Tante Sabine is dead and buried, and this legend's all make-believe," come a tiny voice at my feet.

"It's true as north, Child. Tante Sabine lives on, but she won't bother you none if'n you don't cross her."

When the moon rose high, I ambled home followed by a parade of cats, strays and pets alike. They've been partial to me for years. Just so happens, I passed those two yellow bellied peckerwoods walkin' toward me on the road. I nodded. They cut me a wide berth and kept their bald heads turned to the ground. They'll tell you true if you ask them. They found out the hard way. Old legends never die.

Prime Cut

A woman with five legs sat next to me on the Chicago "L". Two of the legs were hers. The other three were prosthetics, banging, clanging and tumbling their way out of a canvas tote she carried. I tried not to stare, but it was impossible. My eyes kept darting back to those legs - sun-kissed, shapely and life-like. They were fascinating. Concerned that I was beginning to look like a serial killer, I stopped the eye darting and smiled.

"They're broken," she said, as if that explained everything.

"So you cut them off?"

"They're prosthetics."

"Well, that's a relief."

She giggled. "I'm a prosthetics technician."

"Ah, of course," I said, "Let's put your bag over here."

I moved my tool bag to the floor and placed her tote next to me. She'd handed it to me with no hesitation—so submissive, so trusting.

"There, that's better, isn't it?" I asked, peering into her eyes.

She was sexy in that I-have-no-idea-I'm-hot kind of way. Good Me wanted to leave her alone. But her eyes smiled back, flashing gratitude and maybe a hint of something more. I turned Good Me off like a switch. He's such a killjoy.

"Yes, that's much better," she said, with a smile. "You didn't have to move your bag. Thank you, Sir."

But of course I did. Letting Bad Me out of the bag too soon would spoil things. "Sir?" I said, "You're killing me! My father is Sir. Just call me Jack."

"Then thank you, Jack. I'm Amber."

She extended her hand to me, fragile and delicate; mine swallowed it whole. I tried to focus on her face, but my eyes drifted to her legs. They were svelte and flawless, tawny like the legs in the tote. My free hand drifted to the bag and found itself brushing against the cool, smooth surface of one of those legs. A shiver swept my spine.

"The pleasure's mine, Amber. Besides, my tool bag doesn't have anything cool in it like spare legs, so your tote gets the seat."

"What kind of tools do you have?"

"They're for carving."

"Like wood carving? Sweet - maybe I've seen your work in town?"

"Not likely," I said. The thought of introducing her to those tools made me giddy.

Chit chat had served its purpose. It was time to close the deal. "So which station's yours?"

"Ashland and 163rd."

"There's a coincidence; that's my stop. What street did you say you live on?"

"I didn't."

Her voice was flat; the silence that followed absolute. I'd pushed too hard. It was time to regroup.

"Jesus, I'm sorry. That sounded like a come on, didn't it? I'm so embarrassed. Look, Amber, I'm old enough to be your father. All I could think about was how late it is, and how I wouldn't want my daughter trying to make her way home at this hour by herself, lugging a bag of plastic body parts through the south side. There are a lot of creeps out there, you know? I was just trying to look out for you. No hard feelings, right? Tell you what. How about you let me pay cab fare to make sure you get home, okay?"

Good Me had thrown down the gauntlet. He was on a mission to get her home in one piece.

"It's alright. I'll be fine. I'm not parked that far from the station. I can drive home from there."

"Do an old man a favor, huh? Let me walk you to your car. I'll sleep better knowing I got you there in one piece. Your dad would want you to be safe. Do it for him. Please?" Bad Me is such a clever son-of-a-bitch.

She flashed that sweet, hot little smile. All was forgiven. Ying and yang were back in balance.

When the train pulled into the station, I swung her bag o' legs over my shoulder. Bad Me grabbed the tool bag as we left the train. He ran his finger up and down the zipper, stroking its teeth, desperate for the chance to come out and play.

The three of us walked into the darkness. It was anybody's guess which Me would win.

Promises To Keep

After three shots of Cuervo and a pickled egg, I toasted my dead father. It's not like we were close. All he'd left me was a thirst for tequila and assorted broken bones. I flew home to watch them put him six feet under—just to make sure he stayed there. The folks in town were quick to welcome me home. I was quicker still to let them know I'd be taking a flight home in the morning. Some people and places are better left behind.

The turnout at his funeral was small. Acquaintances of my father extended their deepest sympathies. Those who knew him better just nodded in respect. Pastor Givens rambled on about Heaven and the bounty of God's forgiveness, but I figured even God had His limits. It seemed more likely that my father was destined for fire and brimstone. I smiled at the visual, poured myself a double, and leaned against the railing of the overlook at the Cascade Inn. The mist from Richmond Falls sprayed my face. I'd almost forgotten how loud those falls were. God knows over the years I'd tried, but the fury of that water started churning up things better left forgotten. It's odd, about memories. When they break loose, they flood like the first spring thaw. Memories I'd buried twenty years ago clawed through the silt and up to the surface.

Memories that had nothing to do with the heartless bastard I'd just buried—and everything to do with Izzie.

****

"How much blood you think we need?" Izzie asked, blue eyes squinting; nose scrunched, inspecting her pocket knife through a tangle of blond curls.

"I dunno, what'd the book say?" I pointed to a spot of gunk on the knife blade. She spit on it and then scratched it off with her fingernail.

As far as I was concerned, no bloodshed was required, but she'd read some book about blood-brothers and decided it was a fitting way to seal our friendship. She was serious about it, too. Truth was, at ten-years-old there was nobody else on earth I'd have rather been sealed to, and I'd have given her every drop of blood in my veins if she'd wanted it.

"No need wastin' any, I guess." Izzie drew the blade across her palm, making a small quarter inch scratch. "Here, gimme your hand." I hesitated. "You big baby! I'll just nick you, I swear. It won't hurt, I promise."

I gave her my hand. She pretended not to notice the bruises on my forearm. Young as she was, she knew who'd made them though she'd never say. She nicked my palm and then laced her fingers into mine. My heart skipped a beat.

Izzie finished the ceremony with a prayer. "Dear God, George Humphrey Willis here is my best friend. Him, and me, Isabelle Louise Carter, swear to stay together forever, like two peas in a pod. Wherever I go, he goes and the other way 'round, too. We'll follow each other to the moon and back if we have to. And there's no take backs, neither. Thanks for listening, God. Amen."

"Amen." I swallowed the lump in my throat and surrendered my heart. Watching the blood trickle down my palm, I realized she'd been right. It hadn't hurt a bit.

She kissed me on the cheek and giggled. "Now, you have to follow me, George Willis, just like you promised. Let's go walk the tightrope!" She took off running toward Richmond Falls.

"No! Izzie, stop! Wait up!" I yelled, running after her.

By the time I caught up to her, she'd climbed on top of a deadfall of rotted trees stretching across a thirty-foot span of rapids at the mouth of Richmond Falls. I'd crossed the tightrope once before. I'd never do it again.

"Come on, George, follow me!" Izzie picked her way across a third of the deadfall. It groaned beneath her.

"Izzie, get down from there!" I screamed.

"I will not, you big scaredy cat. See, it'll hold us just fine."

****

Standing there at the overlook some twenty-five years later, her voice was as clear as it had been that day; the ache in my heart every bit as real. I chugged the Cuervo straight from the bottle. Hundred-proof truth seared my throat, and I realized for the first time that I hadn't come back to bury that monster. I'd come back for Izzie.

In my entire life, no woman had promised me forever. How could she? I'd never given her the chance. I'd promised myself to a girl with wild hair and sapphire eyes. I belonged to Izzie. She was all there ever was, all I ever wanted—and all I needed now.

Closing my eyes, I tried to picture her sweet face hidden behind a tangle of curls, but all I could see was her bouncing on that damned deadfall.   I heard the sharp crack it made breaking in two and her scream that got swallowed by the waterfall. I watched her plunge further and further down until the water churned her from sight.

"Izzie," I whispered, as a tear slid down my cheek.

She looked up at me from the swirling water below, arms outstretched, pulling me toward her with her bottomless blue eyes.

"You promised me, George."

"I know I did, Izz." My right foot planted on the railing.

"We're two peas," she said, raising her palm that had once joined with mine.

"Yes we are, baby." My left foot joined my right.

"To the moon and back?"

"To the moon and back." I stood on the railing, looking down at the raging water.

"It won't hurt, George. I promise."

"I know. I'm coming, Izz."

As I stepped from the rail and tumbled through the air into Izzie's arms below, I realized she'd been right. It hadn't hurt a bit.

Sadie's Choice

Sadie's voice, small and aimless, drifted through the shadows of her room. "Excuse me, Miss. I see you out there. I'd like extra towels, please. Miss?"

I stood my ground at her doorway, studying her chart. The facts were undeniable. Sadie was an eighty-six year old, five-foot-tall, ninety-five pound Caucasian female, occasionally demanding, frequently confused, and suffering from end-stage emphysema. She'd been my patient for over four weeks, a lengthy stint in hospice. Deprived of oxygen, the synapses in Sadie's brain had become a tangled string of fireworks randomly exploding, scrambling her neural network. As a result, science labeled her organically demented. Sadie, however, preferred to believe she was a guest at a Holiday Inn who needed additional towels.

Entering the room, I heard her lungs racing to suck in air her body could no longer process. "Evening, Miss Sadie. It's Dr. Burkhart. May I help you with something?"

"I should like my bath drawn and the emerald chiffon gown, if you please."

Her voice trailed off, and her eyes drifted away from me—perhaps to revisit a distant memory of ball gowns, affluence, and gentility. Her pulse was thready and inconstant, flickering like a candle that had burned too low. I slid my hand over hers. "Yes ma'am, the green chiffon it is. Where are you off to tonight?"

"Home," she whispered, her fingers working the bed linens over and over again. "He says to hurry. I mustn't be late."

"Who, Sadie? Who's taking you home?" I asked.

"It's Jack. My Jack." She smiled softly. "He's reaching for my hand."

There were no classes in medical school to prepare me for that moment. There were no books that could define it; there were no rules of science that could explain it. Sadie's life was near its end. There were no friends surrounding her, no relatives gently weeping by her bedside—there was only me. I held her hand in this life, even as Jack held hers in the next.

I'd known the journey Sadie would take that night from the moment I entered her room and heard her tortured breathing. I knew because I knew the science of life with all its molecules, atoms, and sub-particles. It seemed that somehow, Jack, in another dimension, far beyond the reach of science, had known as well.

Sadie's liquid gasps came achingly slow. I stroked her hair and whispered in her ear, "It's not polite to leave a gentleman waiting, Sadie. It's okay for you to go. Jack's been very patient."

She lifted her filmy eyes in search of my voice—though they could no longer see, they crinkled as they always did when she smiled. She drew her last breath. When she exhaled, the loves and losses of her life entwined and swept past me like wistful dancers stepping to the strains of their final waltz.

I closed her eyes. Lingering for a time, I pondered what a blessing it had been for Sadie's mind to have created an alternate world that transformed the stark realities of hospice into an innocuous hotel defined by tiny soaps and an endless supply of towels. Perhaps that fantasy had not sprung from her dementia. Perhaps it had simply been Sadie's choice.

Scarlet Sins

There was something peculiar about the old barkeep. His skin was sallow, his gait slow, and his spine more twisted than a hazelnut tree. But he had busy, watchful eyes, discerning eyes that brimmed with anticipation.   It was, I decided, as if he were waiting for someone. I'd been glancing at him from my seat at the bar and noticed that his eyes followed me the way a hawk tracked its prey. There were other patrons in the tavern. Why me?   What manner of mine or lack thereof, fascinated him so?   I wanted to know. That curiosity would cost me dearly.

"Nice establishment you have here. Gideon Thorpe," I said, extending my hand.

"Levi James. Nice to meet you," he replied. His hand settled into mine like a crippled bird. He poured us shots of his 'special recipe', fresh from the still, I presumed.

"Where 'bouts you from, Thorpe?"

"Boston originally, though I've been west a long while now," I said.

We engaged in amiable conversation, in between his barkeeping chores. He kept the whiskey flowing until the moon rose high in the sky. One-by-one, his patrons trickled out the door toward points unknown until only he and I remained. An eerie quiet settled into the bar. A red fly jittered near his hand; that seemed odd, red flies in winter. He poured me another shot and handed me some bread.

"Eat up boy, you look half-starved. Boston, you say. What're you doin' in Oregon?"

"Penance," I said, with a laugh, "I've been a gambler, flimflammer, rumrunner. You name it, I've done it, without an iota of success, I might add."

Truth be told; I didn't have a dime to my name. I couldn't even pay him for the considerable amount of his whiskey I'd been drinking. I changed the conversation.

"What brought you to Oregon, Mr. James?"

"Gold," he said, looking toward the mountains. "Came from Tennessee, fifty years ago, searching for the Blue Bucket Mines. Hell, everyone was. Gold by the buckets, they'd said. But that shiny bitch was always one shovelful away. By'61, I'd had enough. I drove that shovel deep into the ground and told myself, gold or no; it was for the last time. And didn't I find her! Pretty as a two-dollar whore, she was. Swear to God. And very well endowed. I had money to burn. Even did that once, lit a pile right up. Did a lot of other things, too. Some bad, others, worse; a few that haunt me at night. I've got more money than I'll use in this lifetime, and I'd give it all for a good night's sleep." He leaned in close so I could see the jaundice of his skin. "I'm not long for this world. You can see that. I want to meet my Maker with a clean slate." He tossed back a shot. Then his eyes locked into mine. "You a God-fearing man, Thorpe?"

I shooed a cluster of red flies from my bread. "I suspect the Lord would smite me if I answered yes. No disrespect, Mr. James. I must confess that I am not a believer."

James broke into scripture. "'Though your sins are like scarlet, they shall be white as snow.' My sins are scarlet, boy. I've shed blood—more than once. I need them sins white like the Lamb of God, now before I'm gone! You can take my sins away, boy. I'll give you every cent I own if you do that for me. It's all here, under the floorboards, next to the stove. Yours, every red cent." Hundreds of flies swarmed his head.

"Mr. James, please, the flies!" I begged.

He laughed. "What's wrong with you, boy? Ain't no flies in here. Only sins! Grievous sins that need forgiving."

My thoughts had muddled from the whiskey, those flies, and his lunacy. Though reason urged me to flee, something darker bid me to stay. What harm could come in humoring the old man? If he wanted absolution, I'd give it to him. Let him die in peace. Besides, his cache of gold would be mine, for only the price of my indulgence.

He must have read my mind. Pulling his knife from its sheath, he sliced his wrist, bled into a shot glass, and dipped my bread in it. The blood instantly seeped into the bread and congealed.

The droning buzz of wings rose to a crescendo, then bust into a roar as his body exploded into a roiling mass of flies. His voice sprang up from inside the crimson swarm, "Now, Thorpe! Eat, drink. Take my sins. You will have all that I promised and this lunacy shall pass!"

Wanting nothing more, I choked down his trespasses, retching, tasting my own bile as the flies swarmed inside me. They slid past my gullet, deep inside me and the world went black. When

I awoke, I was alone. No sign of James, no flies, no blood, just an empty whiskey bottle and a toppled shot glass. Not for the first time in my life, I swore off the demon liquor.

Apparently, the old man, in his compassion, had allowed me to sleep it off. I shuffled toward the warmth of the stove. The floor boards creaked underfoot and teased loose a memory. The floor. Something about the floor. His promises returned—the gold, the money, his legacy. Temptation ravaged my brain. With the singular purpose of a madman, I tore at the wooden boards, bare hands bruised and bloodied, to claim my fortune, and found… absolutely nothing.

I bellowed at the betrayal and drove my bloodied fists into the floor. It wasn't possible! The notion of me, a flimflam man, falling for the promise of fool's gold? Absurd! Preposterous! And yet, an inconsolable anguish welled inside me for the loss of a wealth I had never possessed.

But it was only when a tiny fluttering arose deep within me that I understood the truest depth of despair. A solitary red fly fought its way up my throat, into my mouth, and emerged from between my lips. In that moment, I knew there would be no escape from my misery, no reprieve from the loss of the soul I'd never claimed. My fate was forever sealed. The scarlet sins had taken flight.

Secrets

I had a secret. I wasn't using my telescope to study the heavenly bodies of space. I was using it to study my new neighbor, Magda Gatto—the languid sway of her hips when she walked, the way her limbs surrendered to the salsa music wafting from her house, the shimmer of her long, black hair in the Arizona sun. I imagined her scent, and the sting of her long, red nails raking my back. Sheer ecstasy. Night and day I watched her, cataloging my observations.

As a psychiatrist, my obsession intrigued me; as a neurotic, my illness diminished me. The line between the two blurred more each day, but the clinician in me insisted on analyzing her behavior.

Magda prowled the streets from dusk till dawn, returning home, hollow-eyed and gaunt—suggesting insomnia, promiscuity, or other self-destructive behaviors. Her frequent showering and grooming rituals, though tantalizing to watch, were clearly compulsive in nature. I wanted to believe her tiny quirks were charming eccentricities. But when Magda returned from her nightly escapades covered in blood that was clearly not her own, her symptomatology escalated to a new level. She was deeply disturbed with secrets of her own and in need of help.

I invited her for drinks. My heart thundered when she arrived sheathed in black - a backless silk dress and fur shrug to guard against the chill of the evening desert air.

"Magda, I'm Tom Garfield. Please. Come in."

As I reached for her hand, I saw a rotting bird corpse cupped between her outstretched fingers; guts splayed across its yellow breast, neck dangling, eyeballs protruding like bloated caviar eggs.

"Jesus!" I said, taking the carcass from her. Strange; she seemed perfectly comfortable holding the thing as if it were a bottle of wine. "Last week it was a rat, and the week before, two field mice. Freaking neighborhood cats. What's next?" I laughed, but a chill slithered up my spine as I discarded the remains.

"Someone's very fond of you, Mr. Garfield, leaving such tasty morsels on your doorstep."

Her almond-shaped eyes were breathtaking - bottomless green my telescope had never captured.

"Mrs. Garfield?" she asked, peering behind me.

"I'm afraid Gerri's stuck at work. She sends her apologies." That was a lie. Though she'd tried to hide it, I knew she'd taken a lover. Ours was a marriage of convenience. "And please, call me Tom.' I handed Magda a glass of Merlot.

"Your home is lovely," she said; eyes scanning, absorbing.

"Would you like the two-bit tour?"

We moved from room to room, eventually arriving at my study, where the telescope was mounted, her bedroom aligned in its crosshairs. How could I be so careless? Freud's theory that there are no accidents flickered through my brain. I bypassed the room, but she stopped, opened the door, and walked inside.

I needed a distraction. "It's nice to finally meet you, Magda. We should have done this weeks ago. People should get to know their neighbors, don't you think?"

"Absolutely Tom, though it seems you've had a head start." She chuckled, resting her hand on the telescope. "Don't worry. I won't tell." She nuzzled my jaw with her nose. "I knew you were watching," she whispered, then flicked her tongue into my ear. "Did you like what you saw?"

She rubbed her body against mine, offering long, wet kisses. We made love—the first of many nights. Her cries were uninhibited—feral; her nails drew blood from my back.

Even in my elation, I couldn't ignore the fractured psyche deep inside her. Each time we met, I tried to exorcise her demons. She was slow to trust me, but patience coaxed her secrets free.

"You'll think my dreams are madness," she said, locking her huge, emerald eyes into mine. "I'm standing in the woods, quivering and panting - waiting for the moon to crest in the sky. My cells begin to ebb and flow; collapsing and regenerating with every heartbeat until I'm reborn as a beautiful, sleek cat. The scent of prey consumes me. Freedom calls and I follow. But at dawn, I awaken in human form and count the hours until night returns, and I'm free again."

"Fascinating!" I said. "Is it a domesticated cat you become?"

She slapped my face. "There's nothing domesticated about me! Want to know the real me?" She hissed, nipped my ear hard, and then whispered what I had already known. "I'm the one who left those gifts for you."

She was acutely psychotic, but the closer we grew, the less it mattered. My desire for her was insatiable. The gouges she'd left in my back burned with infection. Fever ravaged me; the house confined me. I needed space and Magda at my side.

We lived for stolen moments, and the glorious evenings when Gerri was away. One such night, I waited for Magda to come to me. I paced the floor; my passion burned. The hour grew late. Gerri was due to return; yet, there was still no sign of Magda.

An unnerving thump came at my door. I threw it open. There lay Gerri; arms and legs splayed, throat severed, exposing the small, ivory vertebrae at the base of her neck; viscera protruded through a gaping gash in her belly. Behind her stood the love of my life in her truest form - a black and regal panther, tail swishing, and ears peaked, emerald eyes burning for me alone. She stepped forward and washed in moonlight, straddled her magnificent gift while licking me with her long, lover's tongue.

The proof of her passion needed to be scoured from my doorway, but I was already becoming, bones twisting and grinding—organs expanding and contracting. I would have to wash my hands of it in the early light of dawn. Finally, when no human trace of me remained, we raced the wind toward the call of the night - bound in blood, no secrets left between us.

Sometimes

Effie Turnbull stood with a radiant smile in the common room of Tupelo's Fairmont Home for the Aged. The alarm on her wheelchair chirped like a crazed Kildare guarding its nest. Flashing the royalty wave to the other residents, Effie crooned the lyrics to "Stardust" loud enough to drown out the television. She pulled her skirt down to her knees. She wore no slip beneath. A well-worn pair of cotton undies made their public debut.

"Lawdy, Miss Effie! Let's pull your skirt back up, 'fore you get us both in trouble. Look here, I brought you and Miss Enid a surprise today, see?" Nurse Genna Washington adjusted Effie's skirt and pointed to a sheet cake on the game table.

Genna took two candles from the pocket of her uniform and placed them on top alongside the words Happy Birthday Enid and Effie.

"Ah, now ain't that something, dear? How thoughtful," said Enid, rolling her chair up to the table for a closer look. She took Genna's hand. "Don't you let old Effie throw you, child. You know she went 'round the bend, and she ain't coming back. And you,

Effigenia, ought to be ashamed of yourself. No one wants to see a ninety-year-old old hoo-ha anyway. You know better than that. What's a matter with you? Ain't Harvey Jamison paying you no never mind?"

Harvey, the only male in the room, had been scrutinizing the same jigsaw puzzle piece for the last twenty years, studying its shape and admiring its texture, unaware anything else existed.

Effie smiled warmly at Genna and giggled, flipping Enid the bird. Genna snickered. "Which one of you is older?" she asked, dishing out the cake.

"I am, by about ten minutes," answered Enid.

"What was it like growing up back when you were children?"

"Oh, the things we seen, child, so many things! Some big, some small. And there was some things that was big to other people but didn't mean nothing to us. The crash of '29? Well, honey, we was poor before that, and we was poor after. But lots of folks went from having to having not. It was harder for them."

She picked at the cake with her fork, taking hummingbird-sized bites, staring at the icing as if she were watching a distant memory unfold.

"Then there was the big one, WWII, when all the youngens had to go off to war. Lots of them fine boys never made it back home. Thurmond Whittaker didn't. I was kind of partial to him." Her voice dropped to a whisper, and her eyes began to glisten. She paused, caught up in a world gone by.

About that time, Effie flung a fork full of icing at Enid's face and began belting out the words to Heartbreaker, by the Andrews Sisters.

Enid rallied, wiped her face, and chuckled. "Yeah, you right, Effie, he sure was a heartbreaker. You know who else was a heartbreaker, Genna? Effie here. She was always the pretty one, you know."

"You're identical twins, Miss Enid. How could she be the pretty one?"

"Effie had a way about her. It was the shine in her eye, the smile perched at the corner of her mouth, ready to jump out and grab a body. She was a sight to behold--a force to be reckoned with. Filled with life. Not a man wouldn't hanker after her, back in the day."

Effie, uncharacteristically quiet, stared out the window as if captive to her own memories.

Genna reached for her hand. "I'll bet your big sister took good care of you when you were little, didn't she?"

Effie's eyes widened, filled with a long forgotten fear come back to haunt. "It's coming! Sweet Jesus, it's coming, Enid! We gotta hide!"

"Now, now Effie – that was a long time ago." Enid patted Effie's arm. "That was in the spring of '36. A powerful twister raged all the way from Gainesville to Tupelo. A mess of people met their Maker that day. Me and Effie hid in the storm cellar, listening to the cellar doors bounce and groan, watching the lantern flail around, and then blow completely out. We fell asleep in the dark, curled up together, hanging on to each other for life itself. To this day, Effie won't fall asleep with the lights out."

Effie grabbed for Enid's hand, still tangled in the horror of that spring day from long ago.

"I think it's time for you rest now, Miss Effie. I'll take you back to your room and wrap up the rest of this cake for later."

Genna did just that, kissed them both goodbye, and wished them happy birthday.

Enid turned the light on over Effie's bed and held her hand until she fell asleep. Sometimes they didn't need words. Sometimes they only needed each other.

Sometimes There's a Worm

Sometimes there's a worm at the end of the bottle. And sometimes, it eats a hole in your heart.

She stood in the doorway of The Orchid Lounge, glowing, moonlight bouncing off her hair, making me wonder if she was a dream. Maybe it was the lighting; maybe it was the Cuervo. Real or not, she was a looker—blonde, with a set of maracas that could poke your eyes out and the hottest gams since Syd Charisse. Her 'come-do-me heels' clicked against the linoleum, making me think she was the real McCoy.

Dames like her spelled trouble.

Working her curves better than Koufax, she passed a string of empty stools and sat her tight behind next to mine. She gave me the old one—two, with her Chanel No.5 and her baby blues. "Hey Stranger, I'm Betty. What's your name?"

"Manny," I said, giving her the once over; trying to get a bead on her. What did a babe like her want with a mook like me?

"What's a girl gotta do to get you to buy her a drink, Manny?"

One look at her smile, it didn't matter what she wanted. She'd end up getting it. I'd let her play me like a marimba, 'cause mopes like me don't get too many bites at an apple like her.

Inside of a week, she took me for booze, dinner, a shoulder to cry on, not to mention my johnson, and the last, stinking buck in my wallet. But it wasn't enough. She wanted more. By the time I knew how much more, I was so dizzy with the dame I'd have given her my left nut.

"I'm behind the eight-ball, Manny; elsewise, I wouldn't be asking," she'd said. "One of Big Dom's stoolies spilled the beans. Told him I was moonlighting as a canary at The Paradise Club. Big Dom slapped me around 'cause I didn't cut him in on the take, see. He snatched the key from around my neck, for the bus station locker where I stash my valuables 'cause you can't trust the low-lifes in this town. Said he was confiscatin' it in Lou of compensation due. Whatever that means. Who the hell is Lou? Anyways, he hung my key around his neck and left, screaming he'd be back on account of he wasn't done takin' it out of my hide yet."

"Big Dom," a.k.a. Dominic La Paglia, was the wise-guy who pimped Betty and his other fillies out of a cat house at Riverside and 57th. Rumor had it he'd bumped off Lefty Larosa for his sex and drug trades. The wrong goon to cross.

"I got scared Manny, so I flew the coup, but that just made it worse, 'cause I know things. Things he don't want getting' around. He'll sick his goons on me, and before you know it, I'll be pushing up daisies in some scrapyard. You gotta whack him, Manny. I don't wanna die! Please, baby? And get my key back from that no-good palooka. A girl needs her things."

I'm over the moon for this doll, what choice do I have? So, shmuck I am, I go to The Galaxy Club, where the made guys play Five-Card, C-Note a hand on Tuesdays, and wait for Big Dom in the alley. Midnight, he comes stumbling along, scratch pouring out of his pockets like rain. I follow the trail of bills, make sure we're alone, and pump two into his ticker when he gets to his car. I shove him inside, drive him to the North River, and snatch the dough from his overcoat. Then I yank Betty's key from his bulldog neck and salute the no-good bastard as he and his car go for a dip.

Betty turned on the waterworks when I told her I'd plugged Dom and planted him in the drink. I handed her the key.

"Oh Baby, I owe you so big. How can I repay you?" she asked. I told her I'd take it out in trade. Money, sex, freedom – I had it all 'til the coppers nailed me. Funny how they knew where to find Big Dom, and who it was plugged him. Turns out, that locker key wasn't Betty's. It was the key to Big Dom's dope drop. Damned Betty. Put me in the slammer and took it all. She was brighter than she looked.

It's like I said—sometimes there's a worm at the end of the bottle. And sometimes, it eats a hole in your heart.

Stiff Willy

Willy perched on the edge of his bar stool, hungry and ready to pounce. His eyes scanned for prey across the bar. He caught his own reflection bathed in the golden glow of a neon Bud sign and paused in self-tribute. Hail to Willy, The Chick Whisperer; Willy, The Alpha, here at the multiplex bars of the Metropolitan Hotel. He marked his territory with Aqua Velva and basked in the glory of his Willyness.

It was Wednesday, ladies' night, at both the Stardust Room and The Galaxy A-Go-Go. So certain was he of success, he never rented his own room. He merely waited for traveling business women to ask him to scratch an itch in their corporate sponsored rooms. Like shagging chicks in a barrel, really.

Unsuspecting quarry wandered by—an aging blonde, formerly pretty, emitting the sweet lingering scent of desperation. She'd separated from the herd. A drop of drool plinked onto his drink coaster. He wiped his mouth with a napkin, adjusted his toupee and using his signature line, went in for the kill.

"Excuse me Miss, did you know your eyes are brighter than the stars above?" Willy lifted his gaze soulfully to the planetarium-like ceiling of the Stardust Room.

The blonde attempted a girlish giggle that sounded like a cross between a wheezing Lon Chaney and a Canada goose. She batted her false eyelashes.

"Hi! My name's Brandy. What's yours?"

Alpha Willy triumphed again though she wasn't much of a challenge. He had her key to room 321 within half an hour. But he could do better. So he nuzzled her neck and excused himself briefly to visit his dying mother at the nursing home before lights out. He'd let himself in with her key when he returned. She swore she'd wait up. But of course she would. Blowing Brandy a kiss, he strolled to the Galaxy A-Go-Go in pursuit of more delectable game.

****

Victoria had downed three Cosmopolitans in less than an hour. The bartender at the Galaxy gave her a great pour; maybe because she was hot or maybe because she looked like she needed it. Either way was fine. Catching her husband with their neighbor's wife, right before leaving town on business, made death by alcohol sound inviting. But first things, first. Victoria vowed to get revenge by laying the next man she saw. She didn't have to look far. The cheesiest toupee-headed bottom dweller she'd ever seen walked in. She considered waiting for the next guy. But a vow was a vow.

"Hi, I'm Victoria. Buy me a drink, and I'll give you the night of your life." She winked at him, crossed her long slender legs and smiled provocatively, sitting tall so that her breasts strained against the buttons of her blouse.

He leered at her, licking his lips as if she were a ham sandwich. "My name's Willy. I like a woman who knows what she wants, especially when it's Stiff Willy here. What're you drinking,

Vickie?"

Willy? Did he say Stiff Willy? She snorted her Cosmo up her nose. Regaining her composure, she took his face in her hands and shushed him. "Willy, why ruin the moment with words? If you want the best you've ever had, follow me to my room. Just no more talking. At all. Ever."

****

Phil? Bill? Shit, what was his name? Free Willie? Something like that. Victoria rolled over and moaned, bloated from alcohol, regret, and after-sex room service. A vague dread gnawed at her gut.

"Hey ah, Willy Boy, wake up," she said. No answer. "Dude, listen, you have to leave."

Anxious for him to be gone, she shook him so hard he flopped over toward her. His eyes, opened and glazed, were as void as the frozen tundra.

"Oh, Sweet Jesus!" she screamed, slamming her pillow over his face.

Victoria sprang from the bed, tripped over the comforter and sprawled face-first on the floor. Rummaging through his pants pockets, she found his key to room 321. She used the belt from the hotel's courtesy robe to truss Willy like a turkey onto the lower shelf of the room service cart, then draped the tablecloth back on top and rolled him down the hall to room 321. She tucked him into bed naked as a jaybird and then sprinted back to her room. After cancelling her meeting, she threw her clothes into her suitcase and got the hell out of Dodge.

****

Brandy sat poolside sipping her coffee, hoping the morning sun would heal her shattered ego. She'd waited all night for Willy to return. *Such a fool.* She knew a stud like Willy would have loved her and left her. But it would have been the most exciting night of her life. With tears spent, she returned to her room, only to find Willy naked, sprawled face down, resting peacefully in her bed with a room service cart alongside. He'd ordered them breakfast. *How thoughtful!* She smiled in anticipation. *Let him rest for now;* she wanted him primed. It'd been a long time since she'd had a good Stiff Willy.

The Birthright

The Trojan knelt before me drenched with sweat. He refused to meet my gaze, but instead, darted his eyes as if hoping Zeus might rise among the thistle and slay me where I stood.

"Plotting your escape?" I asked. He gulped as the tip of my javelin traced the length of his gullet and poked beneath his chin. "On your feet, slave." He rose with an abundance of caution, coaxed the javelin's tip from his neck and wiped blood from the tangled thatch of his beard. His chest heaved for want of air, and his words tumbled out in staccato.

"Your skills have improved, Amazon. Perhaps I need apply myself more."

"Such bold squawking from the strutting jay! Care to try again?" I jabbed his buttocks with my spear.

"Best leave perfection to the gods," he said with a scowl. "You would not want to anger them."

Myrina, the Supreme Commander intervened with a derisive snort. "Nonsense! Diana is an Amazon. The gods expect perfection from her. Repeat the drill!" She clapped her hands to signal that our banter had ended and cast the Trojan, Agrias, a withering look. "How like a man to rest upon his laurels, and fear perfection. No wonder you tip-toe before the gods! Up with you! And give it your all; else 'tis to the quarry you will go."

"You would see him a laborer?" I whispered. "What of his battle skills? Slave or no, he is still a warrior."

"By the heavens, no! But he must believe that I would. Power, Diana, is in the eye of the beholder. To possess power, one must imply it with the boldest of attitudes lest she betray herself with uncertainty."

"Come, Agrias, once more," I said, with a sigh. "The gods and my commander require perfection."

We resumed our dance, circling each other, two warriors, eyes locked, anticipating every twitch and every tell. I waited for the moment he would pull his shield taught, for a strike toward my head was sure to follow. When it came, I side-stepped and swept his feet from beneath him. He landed on his back with an audible thump and a sharp grunt.

"The gods should be pleased," he mumbled. "As for the commander who can say?"

Myrina stepped over him and came to my side. "Fair enough, Trojan. Retreat to your billet and lick your wounds, though 'tis no shame to be bested by Diana. As it happens, she and I have more pressing matters to attend to." She dismissed Agrias with a wave of her hand and posed a question that I, myself, had often pondered. "Your Amazon sisters are battle-tested, equally matched with Agrias in ability. Know you why I made the Trojan your partner?"

"My sisters learned to fight like Amazons, but Agrias fights like a Trojan. He shows me how men war. Someday, when the moon and stars are so aligned, I will lead our tribe to rise against men and use that knowledge to defeat them."

She nodded her approval. "You are our future, Diana. Your heart is pure and your aim is true. Much as it pains me to say, Agrias is right. The gods should be pleased, as am I. It is time for you to fulfil your destiny and reclaim your birthright."

"My mother died in battle when I was six years old. I know nothing of a birthright."

"So like your mother, Hippolyta, you are," said Myrina. "She longed for a girl child, but the gods would not oblige her. One night, moved by her loneliness, she sculpted you in her own image from the sand, giving you only a left breast for nursing; forsaking a right breast as not to impede your use of the bow.

When she finished her glorious creation, she called upon Hera to bring it to life. And thus, you were born. Hippolyta not only made you a woman; she made you an Amazon. And life without a soft right breast has gained you uncommon strength! So taken with you was your grandfather, Ares, the God of War, that he gave your mother a breastplate said to be endowed with the magic of the gods. It was her most treasured possession.

Upon hearing of its powers, Hecate, the daughter of Hades, emerged from the underworld and stole it from her. That breast armour is your birthright, Diana. Go, reclaim that purloined plate. Make offerings to your grandfather and Athena, the Goddess of War. Pray for their protection. Remember well your training, and when all looks lost, summon that Amazon strength within you, for it will be your salvation."

She reached into her tunic and brought forth a small, well-honed dagger with a single ruby embedded in its hilt. "Take this as well, Diana. It, too, was a gift from Ares to your mother. It is said to come from the temple at Olympus." She held me close for a moment. "Magic or no, at its very least, it is another weapon."

I tucked it into my boot, and allowed my mentor, Myrina, to return home without me, like a heartbroken mother who had delivered her only child unto the world.

****

The shores of Pontus never looked more beautiful, nor smelled more like home than the day my mount, Aithon, took me from their bosom in pursuit of the plate of Ares. Violets, lilies, and larkspur swirled their intoxicating scents around us as they bid safe passage. Aithon, an Andalusian, was gifted to me by Ares in my sixteenth year. And though Ares promised me that Aithon's bountiful heart and mystical powers would see us through the worst of days, thus far, I could only attest that the steed was strong, elegant, and white as winter's snow. Within him dwelled courage, loyalty, and a keen intellect. He knew my mind, my hand, even the touch of my knee on his flank. We rode as one.

He carried me that day along the shore of The Euxine Sea under a cloudless sky, where the temperate sun warmed us both and the scent of brine lured us from our journey to race against the wind and tide. So free were we for a time that we failed to take notice of the sea nymphs, sunning themselves upon the rocky shoals.

"Who goes there?" came a tiny voice. I turned to find a fiery-haired nymph peeking out from between the rocks.

"It is Diana," I called. I'd seen this nymph before. "Halia, daughter of Pontus, is that you? I mean no harm." Aithon sauntered closer, and I opened my hands, palms held high to show them free of weaponry.

"Aye." The timid creature blushed. "A pod of sea nymphs is not much challenge for an Amazon."

"I did not come to challenge you."

"But you have travelled far from the land of my father. What brings you here?"

"I search for the gateway to Hades. I have business with Hecate."

A collective gasp arose from the nymphs. "Brave, even for an Amazon," said Halia. "I know of several gateways though I would not wish to invite the wrath of Hecate by being so... indiscreet."

Our eyes locked. "Perhaps, you would prefer my wrath?" I asked.

"You've no need to threaten us. We are but simple nymphs, not your foe."

"At least, not yet."

'But neither are we friends." Halia's voice grew bolder. "I will help you cross into the land of Hades, but there is a toll for my service, and that toll is payable tonight, with the return of the full moon."

"And what is the nature of this toll?" I asked.

She drew me close with a whisper. "We are having a problem with Dionysius. He returns here with each cycle of the moon; indeed, he will arrive this very night. With each visit, he takes my nymphs at will and offers them nothing in return. He scoffs when the maidens object, and their cries only fuel his debauchery!"

Upon hearing the plight of these docile nymphs, I agreed to Halia's bargain. While waiting for night to fall, Aithon and I reveled in the fresh sea breeze and rolling waves, playing in the surf with the nymphs.

When the sun finally dipped to the horizon, a distant shape could be seen trudging toward us along the shoreline, a jug swinging from one hand and a lute from the other. As he drew closer, a song so garbled poured from his lips that its words were indecipherable. The drunken Dionysius had returned as surely as the stars return to the evening sky. He made straight away for Halia.

"He's such a vile little god," she moaned.

"Well then, who have we here?" asked Dionysius, as I stepped between them.

"I am Diana."

"Ah, yes – the great warrior. I know of you. They call me..."

"No need for introduction. Your reputation precedes you, Dionysius."

"But of course it does. Come to satisfy your curiosity, perhaps? In what way might I… educate you?" An impish grin devoured his face.

"Since you inquire, what gives you such right to rape and pillage these poor nymphs, while giving no thought to equity or recompense?"

"How dare you! I am a god!" he bellowed. "And you, you woman, are unquestionably Amazon, making you the last creature that should counsel me on the niceties of romance. You lie with any man or god you see fit, and when you've had your fill, you'll not take him for a spouse. Indeed, you are more likely to slay him, or condemn him to a life of slavery. What gives you such right to tread upon men as if they were the ground beneath your feet?"

"It is a woman's prerogative," I said.

He wrinkled his brow and scratched his head. "Explain, please."

"Women are superior to men, and therefore, claim dominion over them."

"But I am not a man. I am a god! Think you to test my stones?"

"In truth, you are a demi-god, Dionysius. My mother was Hippolyta, Queen of the Amazons. I am granddaughter to Ares. You may assume that my stones are larger than yours. Or, if you prefer, we could compare." I plucked an arrow from my quiver and raised my bow.

A salacious smile swept his face. "Making war is wasteful, Diana. Besides, you are so much better at that than I. Let your Amazon nature prevail upon me and I will gladly forgo these passive nymphs. Take me, even as I take you! Allow me to sate your womanly urges. I vow you will war with more passion and sleep more deeply, for I will be the best lover you have ever had."

"Still, my beating heart! Surely no woman has heard such words before!" I shook my head at him. "I should think a demi-god would be more skilled in the art of seduction. Have you no less tired sentiments to offer?"

Yet, even as I chastised him, I considered his proposition. He was, for all his arrogance, charmingly rakish and fair of face. But my quest awaited me. "In spite of your thread-bare romancing, I shall take your advice, Dionysius, and allow my Amazon nature to prevail." I moved closer and whispered in his ear. "If you seek your pleasures elsewhere tonight, I shall let you live – for now. Any questions?"

"Plenty of nymphs in the sea, Diana. I'm in no mood for a quarrel and have no need to beg your favors." He dismissed us with a wave of his hand and continued down the beach in search of more easily won prey.

On an impulse, I uprooted a conch shell from the sand "Oh, Dionysius?" He stopped and pivoted on his heel. Hope gleamed in his eyes. "When you return for these nymphs, as I know you will, ply them with gifts and coin, perhaps a gentle word or two. These tender maids are deserving of your best efforts. If you deny them, they have only to blow this conch to summon me. Need I return again, you will not fare as well."

With a well-timed thwack of his rump, Aithon knocked Dionysius onto his bottom. He righted himself and stomped away, sand flying from his feet, hands entreating the gods for justice, and angry words bubbling through his snarled lips. His frame grew smaller as he trekked back along the shoreline.

Halia laughed. "A magic conch shell? Think you he believed that?"

"You pay him too much credit," I said with a wink. "Remember, he is male."

****

We rose the next morning with the sun, ate our fill from the bounty of the sea and drank from the fresh water pools, preparing for our journey to Hades. Halia and her nymphs spun like liquid silk through the rolling waves while Aithon and I stayed our course at the tide's edge. Each step taken and each mile travelled led us closer to the wicked Hecate and the breastplate of Ares.

The shore appeared to be infinite. Surely, it stretched to the very edges of the Earth, and though I knew not where they were, we seemed determined to find them. We passed all manner of flora and fauna, collecting aloe, dill, and berries that could prove useful during our journey. The nymphs were eager to share their knowledge, pointing out groves of aconite and moly. I gathered a sizable collection of aconite stems to fell the larger beasts of prey we might encounter. The nymphs picked moly flowers and ground them into powder for me with their tails, warning me that touching the actual blooms proves lethal to mortals.

Our travels together came to an end when we reached the cave of Hypnos, the next leg of my sojourn to the Underworld.

"Within this cave dwells Echidna, the mother of all monsters. She is our sworn enemy. We shall go no further," said Halia. "Should you survive your encounter with Echidna, at cave's end you will find the River of Death. Go with the gods, Diana. Keep close the herbs we prepared for you. They may be your only hope."

****

Once inside the cave, it seemed to swallow us whole. The air was cold, dank and reeked of death.I called into the void, "Great Echidna! My mount and I seek passage to the River of Death."

A humongous creature with a plated spine, pallid skin, and bulging eyes slogged forth from the bowels of the cave and inhaled so deeply that it gusted the air. "Odd. You don't smell of death." She sniffed again. "Not even illness. What business brings you to the underworld?"

"Hecate stole what is mine. I come to take it back."

"Such courage—or is that foolishness? Either way, your pluck amuses me. I will not eat you, yet. But you must battle my son, the Chimera if you want to pass."

Echidna led Aithon and me deeper into the cave to wait for her son. I soon grew impatient. "Show yourself, Chimera!"

A long, steady growl echoed back. "Are you so disadvantaged that you must hide in the darkness?" I asked.

A thundering roar split my eardrums, causing them to bleed. Then came a bottomless voice. "Oh, I shall take you to the River of Death, Amazon—in little, tiny pieces!"

I felt the monster nearing, smelled his noxious breath as it enveloped me. I drew my sword and taunted him. "Do you intend to talk me to death?" Something slimy flicked my ear; his tongue perhaps? I slashed my sword through the pitch black and felt it connect. A quiet yip followed. "Ah, first blood," I said. Without warning, my legs were swept from beneath me. I tumbled to the ground. Aithon moved to shield me, and to my amazement, from his eyes sprung a mystifying blanket of light!

The Chimera howled at the sudden brightness. I scrambled to my feet and beheld the horror that was the Chimera. His massive head was that of a lion. From his mouth protruded jagged teeth and a flailing serpent's tongue. He had a mutant goat-man torso that tapered to the razored talons of a phoenix. I grasped my javelin with both hands and drove it into the monster, again and again until I had run him through. His high-pitched squeals drew Echidna back into the cavern. As I clamored atop Aithon's back to escape, I witnessed Echidna's sorrow.

"Oh, how you have failed, child, and it has cost me dearly! Your duty shirked, the mortal goes along her way, and I have lost a child."

The Chimera's voice was weak. "Forgive me, mother. I did not choose to fail."

"Better you die now than to face the wrath of your father, Typhos. You were Guardian to the River of Death and a mortal passed upon your watch." With that, Echidna sank her serrated teeth into his neck and tore his lion's head from his mutant body.

At last glance, she lay prostrate across his mutilated corpse, beseeching Zeus for death, filling the cavern with tears that seemed to have no end.

Aithon and I raced to the exit of the cave and emerged into a dystopian world never intended for the living. We hovered, disoriented and bewildered, on the banks of the river Styx. I swallowed the fear that tested me, keenly aware that I had only my wits and loyal steed to deliver me. Sulphur steamed from molten pools that covered the river's shoreline. For a time, it seemed we were entombed with eviscerating heat as our only companion; then, the distant but unmistakable sound of lapping oars reached my ears.

From beneath a shroud of fog, Charon, the ferryman – nothing more than a collection of weathered bones cloaked in tattered robes - slid his boat into the shore and stretched forth his gnarled claw to me. Aithon reared on his hind legs and loosed an angry bellow, kicking at the hideous bag of bones as if to scatter him to the winds. Much as I would have preferred to have given Aithon his head, I pulled at his reigns to settle him, for we would need Charon's assistance to complete our journey.

"Who seeks the service of the ferryman?" he asked. His voice, more vibration than sound, hung in the air like the fog that surrounded us.

"I am Diana, daughter of Hippolyta," I said.

He saw the blush of life in my skin "Only shades may cross. Leave now! You have no business here in the underworld, mortal."

"But, in truth I do. I am here for Hecate."

He flashed a serpentine twist of rotted teeth. "My sympathies. Consider yourself fortunate that I refuse you. Only the properly interred with coinage may pass. You must leave at once."

"You have ferried others mortals, and so, you shall agree to ferry me."

"And why would I do such a thing?"

"Let us wager. If I am victorious, you shall take me to Hecate."

His laugh grated like gravel against steel. "And if I am victorious?"

My eyes met his but found only cavernous voids, the centers of which were small red discs that blazed like lava flow. Petrified lips dangled from his skull, like fossilized worms. Despite the terror bursting within me, I proffered him that which he wanted, above all else.

"I shall take your place as ferryman," I said.

His smelted eyes grew wide. He paused for a moment, and then his frigid fingers grabbed mine. The underbelly white of his bones contrasted with the gleam of a coin encrusted ring that swivelled around his fleshless finger. So near him was I that his sulphurous spittle-flecked my face.

"What is the wager?"

"First, tell me we are agreed," I said.

"We are! Have no fear of that, Amazon. The wager!" he begged

"It is a conundrum. If you solve my riddle, you will be forever free, and it will be I who ferries you to the Elysian Fields."

"Share it now or die!" he screamed.

"Very well. What is it which swallows all before it, all behind it, as well all who watch?"

He stilled himself, eyes closed, and brow furrowed; slowing his breathing as if such effort could birth the answer to my riddle. At length, he began to shake, and his lungs gasped for air.

"By the gods, such cruel fate! How can this be?" he screamed. "I have no answer! Tell me! Tell me now for I am lost and fear that I will go mad never knowing!"

"Honor your wager, Charon. Ferry us safely to the other side, and I shall tell you."

Aithon and I filled his boat to capacity. He took us deep into the river and began to navigate the currents.

"Cast your eyes upon the water, Diana. Tell me what you see."

The water's surface portrayed a series of tableaus. Each scene contained defining moments of my life – the loss of my mother, deeds of courage, and lessons learned in defeat. The scenes swept past with such force that the water began to boil and churn. Aithon pranced as the boat rose and fell to the rhythm of white-capping waves. Still, the ferryman kept us afloat.

"What do you see now?" he asked.

Flashes of iridescent light writhed through the water at frenetic speed. They multiplied ten-fold and hurtled into the air, taking on wraith-like shapes that danced and darted as if stepping to the strains of a silent song.

"What be they?" I whispered.

"Souls," he said. "It is the odyssey of souls—the uninterred and those without passage, those with unfinished business that beckons them—hundreds of thousands of souls! They move through the air in search of the portal that gives them passage back to settle their affairs. And now it is time to settle your affairs with me. We have reached the shoreline. I have honored my part of the wager. What is the answer to your riddle?"

"It is no mystery, Charon. What is it which swallows all before, all behind it, as well as those who watch? It is the only enemy you have—time."

From within him rose an anger that brought the waters of the Styx to roil and foam. In the midst of the tempest, Charon's boat slipped from the bank back into the bubbling murk. As he receded behind the blanket of fog, he loosed a maniacal laugh and offered a prophecy that brought my blood to ice.

"Time betrays us both, Diana. The hound of Hades awaits you."

****

Before us, Aithon and I saw the gate to Hades; an iron fortress so immense that it might have been made for Zeus, himself. It was obsidian, with masterful scrollwork bidding homage to the noble Titans. Ancient Elms towered along each side, in such perfect scale with the gate, that I questioned which of these Titans, god or natural, came first. A quiet hum pulsed beneath my feet. The hum grew to a rumble, which soon became a roar, which built to a cacophony so intense that my teeth began to quake in place. It was only then that the source of the sound revealed itself. A three-headed hound-beast filled the expanse of the gate to Hades. His feet boasted the talons of a lion and his tangled mane flaunted a writhing mass of serpents. At tail's end, he bore a viperous stinger more long that I was tall.

Aithon gave a wild snort and dropped his head. His ears laid back; his foot pawed for purchase in the blackened soil. I held him back with my all, for no training in my life had presented me with such a foe.

"I am Cerberus. What fool seeks to challenge me?" The hound that had been looking outward, far above our heads, glanced downward and upon seeing us released an unexpected laugh. "You? A woman? A single-breasted woman, no less. This is preposterous! Leave me. I grow bored."

Myrina's words returned to me. "If that be your choice then I will gladly leave you—dead, although my quarrel is with Hecate. Take a close look at me, hound. You see a woman with only one breast, but the woman who stands before you is a warrior, possessing more strength and courage than any beast or god. Step aside, or die!" I aimed my bow at his head.

Cerberus twitched his haunches, drove his talons into the ground, and then leapt to the air. My first arrow hit him in the center of his forehead. Though it caused him great pain, he did not falter. To the contrary, his wrath exploded, and he flung himself forward, beyond where Aithon and I stood.

I hastened to notch my next arrow as Cerberus pushed us back toward the iron gate. The arrow found purchase in his left eye, spilling putrid, green pus upon his cheek. With a gut-wrenching howl, he shot his stinger high into the air and brought it down like the finger of Zeus, spearing my beloved Aithon, pinning him to the ground. I fell from his back and careened to the ground with the sound of his death screams ringing in my ears.

I dove across Aithon's back to recover my quiver, and saw that which I had forgotten—the arrows laced with aconite. I reached for them, but Cerberus had returned his attention to me and skewered my calf with his talon. He pulled me toward his crushing jaws and the poisonous shock of snakes that sprung from his neck. I clutched Aithon's mane to hold steadfast and saw his eyes fly open. Gone were the soft brown orbs of my cherished steed. In their place were angry, crimson flames that burned with purpose.

Struggling to breathe, Aithon torqued his body against the stinger's grip and locked eyes with Cerberus. Aithon exhaled, and a gale-force gust of flames burst from his mouth onto the poisonous mane of snakes. While the hound howled and struggled to break free of Aithon, I notched the seven aconite arrows en masse and sent them straight down the gullet of the beast. He writhed as the poison entered his blood stream, destroying first one organ and then the next. Having no time for nature to take its course, I beheaded each of his three heads and in Aithon's honor, impaled them high atop the spires of the gate. I had vanquished the monster. But at what cost?

I returned to Aithon, laid my head upon his chest and listened as his warrior's heart slowed to crawl, and then faded further still. He looked at me one last time as I peered into his face. A tear slipped from my cheek into his eye. His gaze remained fixed, and I knew that he was gone. I wondered if, at the end, he had been watching us frolic on the beach with the nymphs, or nudging me for the apples that I carry in my satchel, or feeling the stroke of my hand on his flank. With its final beat, had his heart ached like mine?

I placed my hand upon his chest and jerked at the hint of movement beneath my fingertips. Surely, that sensation was born of denial and nothing more. Although my mind saw no sense in doing so, I returned my hand to Aithon's chest. The stirring had grown to a flutter, which in turn, strengthened to a beat. Aithon opened his eyes, those gentle brown eyes that so often spoke to me, and in my heart I knew that Ares had been right. Aithon's bountiful heart had not only saved me; it had brought him back to me!

I did not attempt to raise him; rather I bade him drink from my waterskin and spread a poultice of aloe and dill across his wounds. I fed him sea buckthorn berries to return his strength and coaxed him to sleep for a short while. His recuperative powers were amazing, for he stood tall and strong when he awoke.

Together we ventured to the base of the gate. Though I had not seen them before, nestled among the branches of the giant Elms were three winged demons. My patience was all but gone. "I know not who you are, but it was I who killed Cerberus and hung his many heads from the gate posts. Unless you wish to share the same fate, you will not interfere with my business."

The largest of the demons hung by his knees from a branch and flipped feet over head to the ground. "We are the sons of Nyx, the God of Night. Do you know of him?" He stepped forward and ogled me. "I am Morpheus. These are my brothers, Icelus and Phantasos. But we have met before." A dark smirk upended his lips.

Aithon pranced and his mane twitched. Clearly, these creatures did not sit well with him though I had no recollection of encountering them before. The smaller demons kept their distance, hovering airborne, darting like bats in and out of the tree limbs.

"Surely, we look familiar." Morpheus' eyebrows rose expectantly. I studied the demons at length, but my blank expression betrayed me. "Come, come now. You must recognize us!" The irritation in his voice was unmistakable. "Revisit your darkest dreams, Diana. Those dark winged demons that give your heart pause? The ones that shroud themselves in the darkest niches of your mind, skittering on the fringes, always just beyond sight? The ones that awaken you with the coldest of sweats?"

"Ah! Then you are the Oneiroi—the demons of dreams, the bringers of fear." Contempt filled my voice. "So, that is the full extent of you? Frightening innocent mortals when they dare to sleep? Tell me, demon, does it look to you as though I am dreaming now?"

He rolled his eyes, kicked at the sand with his toe and mumbled, "Well, no."

"Then stand aside you puffering jackanape! We are here for Hecate."

Once the shamefaced demons made way for us to enter through the gate, the sky of Hades turned foul. The Elms grew taller, fuller; their branches snaked overhead like an impervious canopy. The ground came to life as a tangle of snapping vines swirled between our feet, tightening with every step we took. Surely, Hecate knew we had arrived.

Aithon and I carefully picked our way among the vines, as if stepping to the strains of an intricate waltz. The last of the light disappeared, and while we could no longer see the encroaching vines, I felt their vice-like grip on my ankle. At that same moment, Aithon shied and nearly fell. The vines and tree roots had encircled us and bound us in place!

The Elm branches bowed their heads and began to thrash us. We were not long for the fight. With vision in the darkness all but lost, I moved my hand along Aithon's flank until I felt the soft, bulky shape of my satchel. Reaching inside, I found my mark, the skin filled with the crushed moly flower prepared for me by the sea nymphs. Its black roots and white blossoms, when pulverized, were the best defense against the dark magic of Hecate. I threw the moly powder into the air, letting it dust the writhing branches and then settle on the ground to still the angry vines. Their grip began to ease. They peeled away from our bodies and scattered like disobedient children. The first of our battles in Hades was won, but what was yet to come?

The fortress of Hades loomed at the edge of the thicket, calling like an amorous beast. Closer we came, and then closer still, until we stood at its watery moat. I studied the trench carefully to know its depth and content. The waters began to bubble and soon frothed themselves into a bloody roux. Within that vile soup played visions – visions of my mother's death in battle, images of Aithon being torn in two by the jaws of a hideous monster, and scenes of my own grisly passing at the hands of Hecate. Fear spread its gnarled fingers inside me.

"Protect me, Grandfather. Protect me, Athena," I prayed. "Give me wisdom to recognize these cruel illusions are born of Hecate's trickery. Give me courage to rise above my fears, reclaim my birthright, and fulfil the destiny that awaits me."

As if in answer to my prayer, the waters quelled. All that remained was turbid brine though the width of the moat was many lengths too far for even Aithon to jump. As I considered how best to cross, Aithon paced several steps back. He twitched beneath my hand, signalling his intent. I held tight as Aithon raced to the edge of the moat and jumped. To my dismay, his feet did not descend. We took flight! We flew beyond the farthest edge of the moat and came to rest on a marble floor at the entrance of a long, pillared hallway leading into the House of Hades.

Aithon's steps echoed inside the hallway. We inched forward, taking time to search each alcove for the dangers certain to be found. Halfway down the corridor, my instinct bid me pause. Hecate was near. A ball of lightning screamed out of the darkness and across the alcove toward me, causing me to fall from Aithon's back.

"Hecate!" I screamed into the void. "Enough games. Show yourself, witch!"

Amid the resident darkness, rose an even more oppressive shade, a free-floating and ominous specter. Once fully manifested, the shade took the form of Hecate. She was tall, lean and winsome in her wickedness. But how bold could this vixen be? She wore the breastplate of Ares! It was then I noticed a ball of lightning resting in her palm like a subservient pet.

"What think you of my armor, Amazon?" She hurled the lightning ball at me with astonishing speed. I dove to the side, drawing her aim away from Aithon. The ball hissed as it passed by my ear.

"Is that the full measure of your power? "I asked. "Sleight of hand and illusion? Surely, the fire that burns inside the great Hecate must eclipse the sparks of the child's toys you lob?"

"Foolish girl! Mustn't taunt a goddess. It never ends well." She stretched her hand toward the castle keep where weaponry hung from the stony walls like readied warriors anxious for the call of war. One by one, the weapons pulled free of their mounts and screamed through the air toward me. I dodged them when I could and used my shield to deflect the rest, but they came at such speed, and with such force, that I could not long continue such labored defense. A new tactic was needed. Myrina's counsel had served me well thus far. Uncertainty would prove fatal.

"Fight like a warrior, Hecate! Stop this gamesmanship. Show me the warrior's heart inside you, that I may appreciate my victory when that very heart is stopped by my hand." I squared myself before her, locked her eyes and whispered. "Or, do you play such silly games because you fear me?"

Hecate flew at me with such force that she knocked me on my back. She grabbed my neck and throttled me with far more power than I had expected. I tried to break free of her but when I looked into her eyes, I saw the souls of the dead whose power fuelled her hands. They were legion and choking the life from me. As my sight grew dim, and mind began to float, I heard Aithon's frantic cries and understood his meaning. I reached inside my boot and pulled forth the ruby-studded dagger Myrina had given me. I jabbed the tip at Hecate's tender gullet, causing her to release my neck at once.

I quickly moved atop her, never taking the tip from her throat. "Relinquish the breastplate, thief, and I shall let you live."

"I would rather die than bow to you!" she screamed.

I lifted my face and beckoned Hades, himself. "God of the underworld, father of Hecate, I summon you that you will know what transpired here today. Show yourself!"

The horizon disappeared and in its stead appeared the looming face of the Titan. He looked ancient, with a tangled beard and eyes more haunted than I would have imagined.

"Who dares speak to the God of the Dead in such manner? What happens in my house?"

"Long ago, Hecate stole the breastplate she now wears, from my mother, Hippolyta. I come today to reclaim that which is rightfully mine. I offered to spare your daughter's life in return for my property. She refuses me, leaving me no choice but to take both my property and her life."

His voice sounded worn. "Hecate, return that which you have stolen. Give the mortal her property and be done with this calamity."

"The breastplate holds magic! I am Hecate, the Goddess of Witchcraft—it belongs to no one, if not me. Do not interfere, father. She is mortal and cannot harm me."

"I am the granddaughter of Ares. Do not test me. I have no desire to kill you, but kill you I shall if you do not stand down."

Hades' voice split the heavens. "Hecate, stop this at once!"

"I will not. Sink your blade into me mortal, for I will not fall. Do it!" she dared.

"You are my witness, Hades. I offered all to spare her. But now, I am done." With a twist of the blade into Hecate's throat, her blood poured out like a torrent of liquid gold. Her eyes, filled with disbelief, fluttered but a moment, and then closed. I tore the breastplate from her limp body, clutched it in both hands and made straight for Aithon.

Hades wailed at the loss of his wayward child. He gnashed his teeth and tore at his hair. "My child! My Hecate is gone!" Tears rained from his eyes like an endless waterfall of grief. They pooled into ponds that grew into rivers, rushing at our feet.

Hades' voice boomed from within the torrent, "Diana! You will pay for what you have done!"

His tears hardened into hail that thundered down upon Aithon and me. We bounded through the rising water and headed toward the gate. Hades' face descended from the heavens; his eyes scoured the current, searching for us. We slid beneath the roiling waters and heard his angry rant. "You cannot hide from me, Amazon. Come, accept your fate!"

The torrent of tears stopped as suddenly as it had begun. We would soon be found. Making one final charge for the gate, we leveraged our bodies against it, pushing with all that remained within us. Even as we tumbled through the gateway, the fist of Hades punched through the heavens like the Hammer of Zeus and pounded the ground behind us. Our footprints, barely made, disappeared into the fathomless void left in their wake. With the wrath of Hades behind us, we rushed to close the gate. Could it be that we had lived to tell the tale?

I knelt in supplication, offering prayers of thankfulness and devotion to the gods who protected us. I removed my Amazon armor and slipped into the breastplate of Ares. The moment that it touched my body, it was infused with a sudden heat. I could feel it molding to me, embracing the singular curve of my chest. How right it felt! How strong I felt!

It was then that Ares appeared to me, not in the form of a god, but in the form of a wizened soul who was both grandfather to me and partner to my mother. He spoke of the true nature of my birthright.

"No breastplate of mine, no dagger from Olympus, no gift in all the heavens possesses a magic that is conferred by ownership. I gave these gifts to your mother because the uncommon strength and courage within her gave them power. Just as the strength and courage within you empowers you. Go with the gods, grandchild. Wear my breastplate well. May it, and your fortitude, always shield you from harm."

Aithon and I began our journey back to the mortal world above. I knew not what heinous obstacles we would encounter, nor what monstrous fiends would challenge us. I knew only that we would be protected — not by the power of the gods, but by the power of the Amazon within me.

The Chamber

(From the Journal of Dr. Wallace Fitzhughes)

7 April, 1870; Baltimore

Dearest Annoria,

Time has not assuaged my hunger for your lips, nor dulled their crimson blush in my mind's eye. Would that I could join your sweet repose, but the beating heart within my chest denies me. The very blood that gives it life is my sworn enemy. Until the gods assign my appointed hour, each day I shall pen missives to you, imagining your journey were of temporal duration; thus can I share with you the inconsequential madness of my daily life, whilst fantasizing your safe and swift return.

Mark me, Love. Monotonous though the day had been, this evening passed like none before.

A most extraordinary colleague sought my services; a man of some means, arriving by private coach. Through the window, by lamp light, I discerned a pall that only grief can paint. His name was Winston Twitchell, an apothecary by trade; his desire, to converse with the dead - inside my psychomanteum.

'A preternatural portal,' he called it.

'An unrealized dream,' replied I.

Mourning the loss of his daughter, Elsbeth, to consumption, he craved one last glimpse of her visage, and perchance, one final embrace. I agreed to show him my creation, the psychomanteum, on the condition that he accept a cruel but absolute truth.

"The chamber is devoid of all but the faintest candlelight. Its walls, ceilings, and floors are draped in black. A mirror hangs mid-wall with a single offset chair. All is as it should be. Many hours have I passed inside, seeking my beloved wife, Annoria - to no avail. It pains me to say, despite my most persistent efforts– it does not function."

Twitchell paused. "I am unaccustomed to begging. Grief robs a man of many things, Dr. Fitzhughes—the least of which is pride. There is no peace for me, no sleep, no care for the future. There is only an ache that swallows me whole. Have mercy, Sir. Is it so much to ask? If I fail in the attempt, what cost to you?"

What indeed? I opened the chamber door, escorted him through the blackened void, and tucked him into the over-sized chair like a mother bird nesting its young. His eyes wide, in terror or anticipation; I knew not which.

Profoundly moved, I grasped his hand. 'Find her,' I whispered, then sealed him inside the black abyss and took my place in the darkened antechamber, watching through a hidden observation hole.

Imagine my dismay when I saw him remove a small metal flask secreted within his jacket! I thought perhaps his nerves were frayed, and he required a strong libation, but when he removed the cap, steam bubbled o'er the top and down the sides of the flask. He took a goodly swallow of the unknown potion before replacing the cap, shaking the remains vigorously before lowering the flask to the floor. Questions consumed me. What advantage would this tonic bring? How was it made? Be still my racing mind- would it work?

He relaxed, stared into the mirror, eyes heavy but unyielding to the shapes and shadows crafted by the candlelight. His breaths grew shallow and less frequent until his chest refused to rise, yet steam wafted from his mouth as happens in winter's chill. Ice crystals etched the mirror's surface; indeed, the outer wall grew frigid; then a blissful glow transformed his face.

'Elsbeth!' Twitchell cried.

He rose from the chair, arms outstretched, embracing the unseen. 'I shall never let you go, Child.' A lone tear, slipping down his cheek turned to ice. His joints popped and cracked like water contracting as it freezes. Before my unsuspecting eyes, his entire body froze en masse. Too astonished to look away, I saw his solidified body topple and sever at each articulation as if cleaved!

I retched. Oh, Merciful God, what had we done? Worse still- what lay ahead? Despite the gruesome scene, I collected myself and devised a ruse for the returning coachman. Upon arrival, I rebuffed him with a fabrication - Twitchell elected to walk home on this warm spring night. Following deliberate calculation, I disposed of Twitchell's remains, lest they be discovered, and accusations fly.

Sweet Annoria, I fear the grip of madness, for the line between reality and fantasy is no more. It is deep in the night, and I am spent. My eyes are weighted with all they have seen; my heart sickened by the unspeakable thing I have done. Pray, my love, that rest, and the rising sun restore hope.

Your devoted spouse,
~W

8 April, 1870

My Darling,

I awoke to a visit from the town constable, prompt in his investigation of Twitchell's disappearance. I held true to my deception and offered nothing further. He tarried unnecessarily, observing me with a keen eye.

Despite my misdirection, suspicion will soon fall on me like a swift sword. I can offer no explanation for the manner of his death, nor would my accounting of the evening's spectral events find favor. May Twitchell's remains mire deeply in their fertile graves, lest my life forfeit.

I envy Twitchell's contentment. Oh, that I could hold you without end! Fear not, my sweet, I shall find you. It is only a matter of when.

Yours,
~W

9 April, 1870

My Beloved,

Comes an angry knock upon my door. The constable returns, sidearm drawn, accompanied by his men. Might some hungry hound have unearthed a grisly treat? Mayhap Twitchell's limbs scratched and clawed their way up through my garden soil to decry their contemptuous interment. It matters not. I know my path of choice.

I'll not await the hangman's noose. The last of Twitchell's tonic passes my gullet even as I write. I return now to the chamber, that bleak and glacial tomb, to feel the frigid rush of death sweeping through my veins - to see you, my love, through the mirrors' icy haze, and to embrace you ever more.

Eternally yours,
~W

The Dead Webb

My neighbor, Mrs. Finkelstein, appeared to be dead. But what did I know from dead?   I was ten years old. She was lying in a coffin, people were crying, and the room reeked of lilies. Dead seemed right—until she ditched the coffin and went vertical in the "Valley of Death" viewing room at Templeton's Funeral Home. That blew my theory all to hell.

She glanced at her burial shroud, then shot me the stink eye, and asked, "Edwina, why am I in this focacta outfit? What? I should look like I'm dead? Where's my Mortie? I need an extra fifty for the tables tonight."

Wide-eyed and stifling a scream, I pointed toward the kitchenette.

"Oooo! Lox and bagels!" She wafted down the hallway like an escaped parade float, searching for her husband and a shmeer. Not a single head turned in her direction - because no one could see or hear her, except me. I remember wondering if there were craps tables in heaven, and if, in fact, that's where she was headed. Considering that she didn't realize she was dead, I wasn't going to ask her.

That's the day I knew I was different. Some people were born to pull the square root of pi out of their butts; some people were born to cure cancer using frontal lobes the size of cantaloupes. I, Edwina Sophia Starks, was born to kibitz with dead people.

Imagine my delight.

****

No one gets to call me Edwina, except my mother and Mrs. Finkelstein. I go by Eddie. And yes, Mrs. F. still pops in regularly. It's been twenty years since she 'recycled' herself, and we're still close. Close? Hell, who am I kidding, she's like gum on the bottom of my shoe.

She shows up with her, "Spirits with Issues" support group, or as I call them, 'The Whining Dead.' I've become a psychic Ethernet cable, connecting the space case dead with the whack-job living. Considering the service I provide, you'd think they'd cut me some slack.

"Edwina, eat something, you're too skinny. Edwina, find a man, you're not getting any younger."

 I'm five-foot-four with a shape somewhere between a Greek goddess and a starving fashion model, depending on the magazine. I've got long black hair, sassy brown eyes, and a killer set of coconuts. I could have a shot at a real live guy. But who has time? I'm too busy waitressing at Ronny's Bite-Me Bistro and riding herd on a bunch of snivelling spirits with unfinished business.

Take Phil Gerabaldi, for example, all five-foot- ten and three hundred pounds of him. He was a regular at the bistro, used to sit at table ten. Sixty-eight-years-old, drank like a Cossack and smoked like a fire pit. He died yesterday and showed up in my laundry room this morning while I was doing my whites. Did he want me to guide him to the beautiful bright light? No. Did he want me to tell Gladys, his wife of forty years, how much he loved her? No. He wanted to make sure Gino Battelli didn't get his hands on the 10K Philly had hidden in his cellar.

"Ten large? Where'd you get ten large?" I asked.

"That ain't germane to the conversation at hand." He snagged a red thong hiding in my whites, sniffed it, and zinged it across the room.

"So help me, Philly…"

"Okay, okay. Battelli had it before I - acquired it from him."

I flashed him the 'God Knows What You Did' look. "Aw Chrissake, Eddie. Battelli's a putz. He didn't pay up. I only jacked my half of the take."

Did I forget to mention Philly and Gino were second-story guys? Well, Gino anyway. Philly couldn't get to a second story with a crane. He was the mastermind of the operation. It's a wonder they didn't starve.

"So, what makes you think he knows where it is?" I asked.

"Gladys and Gino's wife, Theresa, sucked down a box of Chianti a couple weeks back. Gladys's mouth ran like a duck's ass. The blabber-mouth. She never could handle a drink. Now I'm gone, he's gonna come for the dough, that snake. Gladys could get hurt. You gotta stop him, Eddie."

Freaking ballsy, these dead people.

****

So I rang the bell at Philly's house, holding a death casserole, homemade mac-n-cheese with little cocktails weenies inside. Gladys cracked the door.

"Hi Gladys, is this a good time?   I just want to tell you how sorry I am about Philly." I waited for her to let me in, but that wasn't happening. In fact, she was sweating bullets, darting her eyes back and forth, looking real antsy.

"Thanks, Eddie, that's real sweet of you. I'd ask you in, but I got a headache. You should go now." She started to close the door.

But Philly screamed in my ear, "Gino's here! He's got a gun on her, the S.O.B.!"

So, I threw my shoulder into the door, knocking Gladys on her ass. I flew right over her, tripping on her outstretched leg, body-checking Gino, and slamming his face with the casserole dish when we both hit the floor.   His gun went airborne, turning end-over-end, then crashed into the archway and fired. The bullet ricocheted off the closet door, through the front door jam, into the window frame, and burrowed into the mac-n-cheese, before busting my casserole dish into bits. Shit! That was my best Pyrex Portable!   Gino pissed himself and was picking Pyrex off his face, but he was still in one piece.

How many people can say their mac-n-cheese is thick enough to stop a bullet? I grabbed the gun and sat on his scrawny ass till the cops showed up.

Eddie 3, Gino 0.

****

Gladys, thrilled to be alive, gave me $1,000 from Philly's stash—small bills, non-sequential, of course. When I was finished rolling around in it, I opened my own business, Afterlife Communication Management Experts, a.k.a. "A.C.M.E. Paranormal

Services, Inc."

Business is good. All I needed was one satisfied customer, Philly, to take me viral on the 'dead-web'. My life turned on a dime. No more slinging hash in The Bite-Me Bistro. And no more freebies for Mrs. F. or her bat-shit crazy cronies. Business is business; that's my motto. Nothing personal, but you give the dead an inch—they'll take a mile. That's just the way they are.

The Devil's Due

A soul is a dear thing to lose—if you hold such beliefs. But the time comes when we all must pay for our sins. I was young and free spirited in '31, preferring both my liquor and my men one-hundred-proof. Having traded sweet tea and soirees for sour mash and speakeasies, I assumed my soul was already destined for perdition. But I was sorely mistaken. Damnation isn't so easily achieved. It takes the devil himself to claim to a soul. And the night he came for mine, he took my breath away.

****

I stood on the balcony of Lamar Thibodaux's plantation house, staring down the oak-lined lane that led to Missionary Road. Music from the ballroom drifted into the sultry night air. My curls, damp and loosened from endless dancing, clung to my cheeks. I fanned myself, finding no relief.

A velvet breath caressed my ear. "Might I be of assistance, *Mon Cheri?*"

I turned to find the most beautiful man I'd ever seen, tall, sleek, and broad shouldered. He was swarthy with hair so black it shone indigo in the moonlight - his face exquisite with chiseled features and eyes the color of the ocean. But it was his smile, so perfect and self-assured, that made me forget to breathe.

"Perhaps this will relieve your distress," he said.

I lifted my hand expecting his handkerchief, but instead, he plucked an ice cube from his drink and placed it at my throat. His fingers feathered downward across the swell of my breasts. He lingered momentarily, eyes embracing the fullness of my curves. He let the melting chip fall from his fingertips and slip down my cleavage. I shivered as it slid across my skin, but did not pull away. He was reckless, brazen, and utterly captivating.

"Forgive my impertinence, Madame. I sought only to ease your discomfort. I am Lucien Beaumont. And you are?"

"Charmed, I assure you, Monsieur Beaumont. My name is Allison DeChamps. *Enchante.*"

Warmth consumed me as he touched his lips to the back of my hand. "The pleasure is mine. Perhaps Madame would care for a drink?" he asked.

"*Absolument*! Whiskey please, a double on the rocks." I fingered the icy trail that lingered on my neck, gazed into his eyes and whispered, "Make that extra rocks."

****

I hastily excused myself from Lamar's party feigning exhaustion from the summer heat. A chivalrous southerner, he escorted me to my suite and bid me goodnight. After removing the comb that pinned my hair, I flung wide the doors to the veranda. Thunderheads roiled across the sky. A blustering wind wafted my hair and billowed the white summer sheers that covered the balcony doors. Lucien stepped through them, crossed the room, and took my mouth in his.

Lightning flashed; thunder rolled, ebbing and flowing with the tides of our passion. He anticipated my every desire, my every need. I ached for his touch as I had never ached before. Though skilled as a lover myself; I had never known such passion. Having given him all, still I craved his caress. We lie, spent, languid, watching the lightning as it snaked across the sky.

He gazed into my eyes, tracing my lips with his finger, and asked, "What is it you want most?"

"To enjoy this moment forever," I murmured. Lightning seared the night sky. I thought it an illusion when his eyes turned black as pitch.

"Tell me, *Cheri*. What would you give for such an eternity?"

****

That was eighty years ago though the reflection in my mirror remains the same today as it was then. Some things have changed while others have remained the same. Southern nobility has faded, and speakeasies have evolved into martini bars. I still prefer both my men and my whiskey one-hundred-proof, though I confess, I've little in common with what passes for a gentleman these days.

Lamar and my other cronies have long since left this world behind. Sometimes I visit the old plantation house and revisit the memories of that carefree life. There are other more recent memories to dwell upon, but none so sweet—nor any that I would be entitled to under the laws of natural order. We are not designed to live forever.

On occasion, Lucien still comes in the night and takes me with abandon, though he no longer disguises the hideous monster within him. His elegant features and bedroom eyes are secreted behind a ghastly, wicked countenance. He is rough and horned and vile. I close my eyes as he ravages me to recapture memories of the handsome rogue who stole my heart that night.   But he will never return.   There is only the devil who seduced me for my soul.   And payment is due – ad infinitum.

The Goddess of War

Dr. Klatua wasn't dead—yet. But ten minutes into my session, the only thing keeping me from killing him was the Heja Root I'd smoked earlier in space dock. He was a typical Martian, four-foot-ten, reptilian green with scales here and tentacles there. His voice was shrill and warbled like an Aldarian Loon.

"Bibi," he said, "Earth women have a hard time adjusting to marriage here on Mars. What you're feeling is completely normal. Embrace those feelings. Own them."

"Maybe you didn't hear me right, Doc. I said my husband, Asshat, wants another wife; two wives—at the same time."

"That is his right as a Martian - Mormon hybrid, Bibi."

"But he's invoked Rune-Pfar!"

"And how does that make you feel?"

"Like I'm not really in the mood for a death match. Thanks anyway." A bronze figurine of Mensuc, the Martian goddess of war, mocked me from the coffee table.

"Rune-Pfar is dangerous, Bibi, but at least Asshat is giving you the opportunity to fight for him rather than to share him with another female. Accept your fate whatever it may be. With acceptance comes peace."

"Seriously? I'm paying you two-hundred-fifty fuel chips an hour, and the best you've got is it sucks to be you. Try not to get vaporized?"

"Such a willful and impertinent Earthling! You have never assimilated into our culture. If you choose not to listen, there is nothing further I can do for you. Our session is over." Klatua dismissed me with a wave of his hand.

"Assimilate this, Moron!" I grabbed the figurine of Mensuc, hurled it through the air, and nailed him in his nardroids. Oddly, I felt better.

He cupped himself with a tentacle, glared at me through the tears welling in all four of his eyes, and scrawled ANGER DISPLACEMENT in bold letters across my chart.

"I can see that!" I said, snatching the figurine on my way out of his office.

Halfway back to space dock, the distant thwack of a slamming door and a quavering curse reached my ears.

"Die Earth bitch!"

So much for psychobabble.

****

My star runner was a Condor XL, cerulean blue, and fully loaded with holographic G.P.S, antimatter hyper-drive, and fine Corinthian leather. It was one of a kind, like me. From Earth, also like me. Not so long ago, Asshat found us irresistible. We sat frozen in space dock, waiting for me to stop crying. Damned tears.

I glanced at the figurine riding shotgun in my jump seat. I wasn't sure why I'd taken it. The real Mensuc was a hardcore badass, strong and certain—everything I needed to be. And she'd have smacked the crap out of me if she saw me crying. Maybe that's why I brought it along; so if I started feeling like a wimp, I could smack myself with it.

I lit a spliff of Heja Root and inhaled so deeply it swirled inside my soul. Screw Rune-Pfar and screw Asshat. If my destiny held danger, it would be a danger of my own choosing—and not the whim of a Martian - Mormon hybrid who knew nothing of love.

I nudged the Condor into open space and gradually set her free. Mars and Asshat disappeared into the black abyss of the wake I left behind. A boundless blanket of stars stretched before me like a lighted path to freedom. At the end of that path lay the Novarian Frontier. It seemed as good a destination as any. I slipped the Condor into hyper-drive. Mensuc and I had worlds to conquer. I glanced over at the jump seat. Damned if that statue didn't have a smile on its face.

The Good Life

Fate is a seriously twisted bitch. Why else would she put me in a fight at Morrie's Pub at two in the morning? Here I was on the run, again, with rain pouring down like banshee tears. I wanted to put some distance behind me, but the roads were slick. Lying low made more sense. There was a light maybe a couple hundred yards west. Off road looked like the best choice—until a wolf ran out in front of me. I swerved, laying my Harley down in a stinking gravel patch. I was busy counting body parts and picking pebbles out of my skin, when a voice came out of nowhere.

"Some spill, kid."

My head spun around so fast it damn near fell off. Some old dude, ugly as sin, was standing right next to me. He grabbed my hand and yanked me to my feet. We were face-to-face, his eyes locked onto mine. Then he started sniffing long and slow. The corners of his mouth twitched.

"The steamed clams at Wharf 61 are good, aren't they? Me, I prefer meat, warm and juicy."

Freak. I took a step back; my knees buckled. How could he know I ate clams?

"Careful there, Mike. See the light over that rise? That's my place. Let's get you there and clean you up."

"How'd you know my name?"

"It's on your jacket," he said. His mouth grinned, but his eyes forgot to join in.

He hauled me there through knee high brush and plopped me into an antique aluminum lawn chair with moldy, green nylon webbing. We were under a makeshift lean-to butted up against his doublewide. A blazing trash barrel wafted heat my way. I was soaked to the bone. It felt good.

He handed me a cup. "Here you go, kid. Take a big swig. It'll cure what ails you."

Toxic fumes singed my nose hairs. "What the hell is this?"

"Home brew. You'll like it. It'll take the burn out of that road rash."

I figured what the hell. Bottoms up!

"I'm Charlie Two Socks. Welcome to my hunting ground. Anyone you need to call? Anyone missing you about now?"

"No man. No one's missed me in a whole lot of years."

Charlie smiled. His lean-to was plastered wall to wall with dream-catchers.

"Bad dreams, old man?" I asked.

"Never."

"So where're the rest of your people?"

"Afraid I'm the last of my kind, around here anyway." He had a weird look in his eyes. "How you feeling, Mikey?"

"Wicked-good man." And I was—warm, relaxed, half drunk. He was right, that drink was good shit, but it was gone. He refilled my cup. "Charlie, you trying to get me drunk?" *Think you're gonna roll me, old man?*

He leaned forward with a crazy, twisted smile. "Ever wonder what it's like to be free, Mikey? Really free, like a bird or an animal, like a wolf—strong, fast, fearless? Taking what you want when you want it, being in control?"

"What are you talking about, old man?"

"Shapeshifting, dude. Freedom, power, domination. It's a rush."

"You been drinking too much of your own hooch." *Freaking nut job.* I shook my head then drained my cup.

Charlie poured another, winked and shouted, "Atta boy, Mikey, drink it all up 'cause now it's time to howl!"

He walked into the pouring rain, sauntered really, arms swinging free, legs striding slow, confident. He turned to face me. Lightning flashed, and I could see his eyes had gone blood red. The rain steamed off his body in a swirling haze. Thick fur covered his skin. Then there was this ripping sound. Sure, his clothes were busting apart, but it was a different kind of ripping sound, a sick, nasty muscles tearing and bones breaking kind of sound. His joints were twisting, grinding, and separating. When they snapped back together, there was no sign of the old man—just a two-hundred-pound wolf, sitting on his haunches, waiting for me to make a move.

We sized each other up. I had to admit, Charlie made a bitchin' wolf—huge, sleek, and fearsome. He was jet black, so black he had that midnight blue tint, except for patches of white fur on his front legs. Ears laid back and hackles raised; he bared his teeth. A low growl hummed in his throat.

I tried to scramble out my lawn chair, but hey, I was hammered. I fell flat on my face, pulling that antique aluminum piece of crap lawn chair over on top of me. Charlie lunged and bit my forearm. I closed my eyes waiting for the kill, but it never came. When I finally did look, Charlie was gone. His bite had barely broken my skin. The last thing I remember was laying on my back under the lean-to, listening to the rain drumming on the roof, and staring up at the dream-catchers, praying they'd work, that this was all just a bad dream—and that I wouldn't wake up dead.

In the morning, I woke up to find the old Indian staring down at me. God, I felt great! And hungry. An insanely good smell, even better than coffee, got me to my feet. "First hooch and now breakfast. You're okay, Charlie. That hooch was kick-ass! Man, the dreams I had! What smells so good anyway?"

"Fresh meat, kid."

Whatever it was, I wanted it bad. Drool slid down my chin. "Bacon, sausage, ham?"

"Something like that."

"I could get used to this life, good hooch, good eats. Hell yes!"

"Stick around. I'll take you hunting with me tonight. Show you the ropes."

"I know how to hunt."

"Not like me."

"Awesome. Count me in."

We walked into Charlie's trailer to chow down. His crazy, lopsided face looked happy. Lonely old coot. I thought. He likes having me around.

Dead Reckoning

The Pecking Order

"June, sit up straight. Lands' sake, hold your head up; let me get a look at you." Momma, with a Lucky hanging out the side of her mouth, eyed me with despair. "Can't you do something with that mop on your head? Geez, June Bug, smoosh it down. You need to make a good impression on Aunt Tillie."

Roy Acuff crooned from the radio of Momma's '37 Desoto. I turned up the volume, hoping to drown out Momma's voice but didn't.

"You want a roof over your head while I'm gone, don't you? Besides, June, she's all alone."

"She's a Holy Roller."

"A little curchin' wouldn't kill you." Momma punctuated her plea with a slow, deliberate drag on her cigarette.

I was only ten-years-old, but we'd played this game many times before. She was much better at leaving me than I was at being left behind. Usually, her leaving was tied to some drunken bum. Choked from the billowing smoke and her dime store cologne, I pulled away and scampered out the passenger door, coming face to face with Aunt Tillie. I sized her up, preparing for battle. She looked wily.

"Who're you?" Tillie asked as if she'd just discovered some new kind of insect.

It was show-time. Momma took center stage.

"Aunt Tillie, It's me, Addy, Digger's daughter, remember? My, look at that flowing black mane of yours! Stayed trim as a hummingbird you did." Momma yanked me in front of her like a human shield, announcing, "This here's my daughter, June. I call her June Bug, get it?"

"You're who?" Tillie's eyes narrowed.

"Addy—your brother Digger's daughter?"

"You don't say," Tillie drawled. "How is Digger these days?"

"He's dead, Aunt Tillie, going on three years now."

"I didn't know. We wasn't real close," Tillie said, but she looked sad, like maybe a stray memory of him had skittered through her mind. She shooed it away with a blink and asked, "What brings you here?"

Momma winked at me and ran her mouth ran like a duck's ass as she walked Aunt Tillie into the house. I knew not to follow. Sitting on the porch steps, I wondered which cockamamie hard luck story she was feeding Aunt Tillie. She had a slew, each one more pitiful than the last. She must've picked a whopper 'cause Momma came back outside bawling crocodile tears, kissed me, and drove off, leaving Aunt Tillie and me in a cloud of dust.

Accustomed to being dumped, I knew I had to establish a pecking order, so I carried my raggedy suitcase inside, flung it on top of the bed, and sprawled face down across the mattress. After spilling a few well-practiced tears of my own, howling some gut-wrenching sobs, I peeked at Aunt Tillie. She wasn't buying my act.

"That there's my bed, little girl, and I don't share. You get the sofa." She glared at me and pushed my suitcase on the floor. A grin tugged at her mouth. "Come along now, we got chores to do. It's time you met Hester."

****

"You want me to put my hands where and do what?" I shrieked. The cow fixed her bloodshot eye on me, and Aunt Tillie nearly had apoplexy laughing.

"Sit on the stool, child, and earn your keep. Hester don't bite, but best warm your hands first 'cause she's got a real mean kick."

"No, I won't!" I screamed, "I won't touch that ugly old cow; I don't want to earn my keep. I don't even want to be here!"

"Your momma didn't give you much of a choice now did she? This is my house—my rules. Milk that cow—now!"

I ran out of that barn all the way to Hoptown, about five miles, trying to escape everything—Tillie, the shame of being dumped like garbage, and feeling worthless. Dust from the dirt road dried my tears. By the time I got to town, my lungs were sucking air like a Hoover.

Plopping down hard on the steps of McCoy's General Store, I tried to figure out how the pecking order got so upside-down. Tillie was a sturdy oak that wouldn't bend. I'd never seen that before. I sat a good long while, long enough that the sun burned low in the sky, and long enough to hope she was what I needed. I had to go back and face her, even if it meant having to cut my own switch.

I walked through her door long after dark. She was wrapped in a worn-out shawl, rocking by the fire. She got up, took a plate from the oven, and put it on the table with a cold glass of milk. I gobbled it down. She licked the corner of her apron and wiped the grime off my face.

Peering deep into my eyes, she asked me, as solemn as a judge, "Do you know why geese always fly in a V?" I shook my head. "It's 'cause there always has to be one goose in the lead—the one in charge. I'm the lead goose in this here family, June Bug. That means you do what I say. You remember that, and we'll get along just fine."

"Yes ma'am," I whispered.

"Geese are loyal, they mate for life, they die to protect their nests, and they never, ever leave their babies. She hesitated and softened her voice. "Your momma, she's no goose, but I am. I'm staying put, right here with you." And that she did, until she died some thirty years later.

Momma never did come back. Who knows why? After a while, it didn't matter anymore. Time and Aunt Tillie had a way of putting things into perspective. It's funny, after all these years, remembering how I thought the pecking order didn't turn out quite right. It's even funnier how it did.

The Prodigal

My memories of her are threadbare—the lilt of her laughter enchanting my ears, the tang of berries from our baskets stirring my tongue. To this day, the scent of the lilacs I picked for her surrounds me. They were a meager tithing for a mother's love more enduring than life itself.

Something caused me to leave though the reason escapes me now. How long has it been? My time away seems both the blink of an eye and the span of a lifetime. It's odd that standing in her doorway, I cannot recall a single event from my absence. Where did the time go?

Regret brings me back; desire to fill the void I left. She is weak and her time is short. I move in close, watching in silence, unsettled by the changes wrought by time and illness.

She wraps her wraithlike arms around her body as if shaken by a chill. The belligerent curls I remember hang bedraggled and dull. Her eyes that once danced like starlight on the ocean are vacant. The enigmatic smile of a mother gazing upon her daughter is gone. Because her daughter had gone. So very long ago.

"Mother?" I whisper.

She turns and fixes me in her abject stare. But she is silent.

"Mother—please!"

She pauses and cocks her head as if to reconsider. I rush to her side, enveloping her in my arms.

"Forgive me." I kiss her velvet cheek.

She closes her eyes, brushes her fingers across the skin I kissed and tilted her face upward. She inhales the air between us with long, shallow pulls and smiles. Tears, sparkling and round, spill from her eyes; first one tear, and then another, followed by a gentle stream. Her trembling hands lift a photograph from her nightstand and hold it to her breast. It is a picture of us, fingers entwined, walking through a sea of purple blooms.

I slip my fingers between hers, feeling the waves of sleep subdue her. She finds my gaze and breathes her last. The stars have returned to her eyes. We find ourselves at play in a field of lilacs.

And I whisper, "It's time to go home."

The Root of All Evil

When the Mortweeds began to talk, Harry pretended not to hear them. They were new to the swamp, skulking among the Sawgrass, wagging their wicked tongues like old crones.

"Better the bastards not know I'm onto 'em," he'd said. "They ain't right, keeping to themselves, not mingling with the others. They's up to something."

For those with an ear, the swamp had its own language; with rhythms, cadence, and pitch. It sang each day like a choir, in happiness, sadness, sometimes even anger. But not the Mortweeds.

"Screech like an un-tuned fiddle, they do," Harry said. "Can't make out they words, but I know they's evil." He pointed at me. "Might just need those herbs of yours, Rowena. They're gonna test you. Best be ready."

"Where you suppose they come from?" I asked.

"Where all evil comes from—the left hand of God," he said, scurrying away, shoulders hitched high; head a-swivel, searching for the mayhem he was certain would come.

Right hand, good; left hand, bad. Seemed to me, God didn't cotton much to grey. Maybe believing in the power of God gave Harry peace. Me? I figured that good and evil came in shades. Evil grew just because it could, taking root in the grey of things. It'd be silly to ask God why He'd smite us with the Mortweeds. Ain't nothing murkier in this world than the greyness in people. What I needed to know was how to kill the damn things. No point in asking the ambidextrous Almighty. I'd figure it out on my own.

Harry met up with whatever it was that came from God's left hand later that night, at his shanty in Kitchimee Bog. Somehow his screams reached out across the swamp and echoed in my brain; I felt his fear gnawing at my insides as the Mortweeds sawed like tiny razors through his skin and then digested him a little at a time. The more they ate, the stronger they grew.

With Harry's screams still ringing in my ears, I headed straight for Kitchimee, herbs in hand. I was surprised when I got to the edge of the bog. There was Harry, pale as a corpse and covered in blood, but standing before me, waiting to be saved.

"I'm coming, Harry! Hang on!" I yelled.

The Mortweeds had worked themselves into a frenzy. Their screams came faster and louder until my eardrums damn near bust. I covered myself with juglone paste to keep them away from me, and started toward Harry, creeping through those weeds, ready to jump if they attacked. But the weeds pulled away from me as I walked deeper into the thicket, at least until I got to its center; there, the Mortweeds twirled around my legs and pulled me down, slicing at my skin, sucking my blood like an army of leaches.

I looked at Harry and screamed, "I'm almost there!" But he wasn't moving anymore; then I saw the tiny bands of weeds wrapped around his arms and chest, holding him upright. He was long dead. They'd used him to draw me in.

I struggled against them, twisting and turning, trying to break their grip, but the harder I pulled away, the harder they sucked. I got weaker and watched in wonder as my blood filled the tiny veins of the Mortweeds, turning them blue with life. I got colder, too, and soon stopped fighting all together. My mind drifted toward the warm, liquid darkness that called to me. I turned my face to the sky, hoping to see the right hand of God reaching down to deliver me. But all I saw was grey.

The Summer of My Father

It was the summer of 1990. My concept of time was based on the stabilities of my life—play time, dreaded bath time, and bedtime—natural enough for a five-year-old. Time even appeared to stop when my father, atop his Harley, nicknamed the Midnight Express, pulled me in my rickety wagon, around and around our yard in ever-growing circles. It seemed we flew at the speed of light; the rush of the wind against my tangled hair and sunburned cheeks blew the August heat away from my grimy sweat-soaked skin.

I knew during those magic rides that my daddy belonged to me. And I to him. Ritual defined that magnificent summer—ritual as pure and constant as my father's love.

One particularly glorious day it seemed as if our ride might never end. We flew with a passion so intense it felt like we were spun into two halves of the same whole. When the last rays of sunlight filtered through the gaps in our tall wooden fence, my father turned off the engine, whisked me from the wagon to the roughhewn fence, and sat down, cocooning me in his massive arms. Tears caught by the setting sunlight shone like diamonds and slid silently down his cheeks. Capturing a single tear on the tip of my pudgy finger, I stared, mesmerized.   I'd never seen him cry.

"Punkin', I have to go away for a while." His wavering voice rocked my tiny world.   "America needs me to make something right in a place far, far away."

"Further than Grandma's?" Surely, there was no place further than Grandma's.

"Yes, baby. It's so far away I won't be able to take you on our magic rides or tuck you in at night for a while.   But you and Mommy will stay right here and wait for me. I love you more than anything in the whole world."

"How many rides will you be gone, Daddy? How many bedtimes?" I asked.

"Oh, don't you worry about that, Punkin', time has a way of flying just like we do on our magic rides. I'll be back before you know it."

Fly as time might, its wings were not destined to bring my father back to me.   And now, nineteen years later, my concept of time is not so very different from what it was back then. When I close my eyes, it is still 1990. My father and I still fly like the wind in dizzying circles, weaving an eternal web of utter and complete love. It is still the summer of play time, dreaded bath time and bed time. It is still the summer of my father.

The Transmogrification of Gordon Giblet

Particularis Industries specialized in molecular amalgamation. Whatever that was. I didn't really care. I only knew some rich bastard was willing to pay me a shit-load of money to steal its data. Screw the chemical engineering of "all natural spit-flavored" denture adhesive and the latest pheromone enhancer for crotchless blue jeans. I was in it for the money – hijacking files and pretending a dollar sign chased the data across the monitor like a starving Pacman.

I'm Gordon Giblet, and that's what I do, or at least, what I did.

But it was different with Particularis. Curiosity was eating me alive; I slowed the download to read the files. Words like hybrid cross-mutation, cellular redistribution, and my personal favorite, genetic transmogrification painted disturbing visuals. I mean, molecular amalgamation? Really? What in the hell were they making? And why?

I smelled a conspiracy.

Recon work needed to be done, but things could get ugly, and waking up dead wasn't on my bucket list. So I listened for the voice from the little guy that lives in the back of my brain—the one who's supposed to say, "Don't do it, Gordo—big mistake." Well, he wasn't talking, the freeloading bastard. Not one to over-analyze things, I took off balls-to-the-wall to save the world from molecular amalgamation without a single plan in my head.

That almost never works.

****

No one would ever describe me as catlike. All five-foot-nine and one-hundred-ninety pounds of me strained, pushed, and squeezed my way through a basement window of the factory like shit shimmying through a constipated colon. I'd already hacked my way past the security system so, once I was in, I was good to go.

I followed my flashlight to the loudest trumpeting, mewling, screeching, every-animal-in-the-zoo-in-heat-at-once kind of sounds I'd ever heard. They grew louder and louder until I swore my eardrums would burst. I'd made it to some kind of containment center. There were stalls that looked like jail cells... with things in them. Things I didn't want to see. But that's why I'd come, right? So I sucked it up and took a long, hard look. Holy crap!

I don't know if they had scientific names, but if it were up to me, I'd go with Maximus-Uglius-Croco-Raptors and Spidiferous-Crawlius-Thingi. Antennas, tails, and johnsons grew out of these things every which way. But shit the damn bed, Louie—they all had human heads! I got hot and sweaty. My heartbeat hammered in my ears. The room got blurry and started spinning. I went down for the count.

****

When I opened my eyes, I was on my stomach, staring at the steel bars of a cage with my hands tied behind my back. A voice took me by surprise.

"Good evening, Mr. Giblet. We've been expecting you."

I rolled over to see who'd spoken. I even banged my head on the floor twice to be sure I wasn't having a nightmare. There, in my cell, towered a giant anaconda, wound into a five-foot wide coil! Enormous centipede legs twitched alongside the entire length of its body. Each of its legs ended in a hand with long, skinny fingers and an opposable thumb. Its human head had bug-eyes. It looked a lot like Don Knotts.

"Who and what are you?" I asked.

"I'm Smythe Slitherquick, owner of this facility and, coincidentally, the purchaser of the data you stole. I assure you I'm human, I'm just... genetically enhanced."

"That doesn't make sense. Why would you hire me to steal your own data? And, dude, whoever told you that you're genetically enhanced is not your friend."

"Mr. Giblet, I don't need to buy my own data. I used it as bait to lure you here. You couldn't resist the challenge. That's what I need, humans with exceptional intellect. Humans like you."

"Damn straight!" I said. Jesus, whose side was I on?

"The next phase of our evolution requires the molecular blending of human cognitive reasoning with the artificial intelligence of a computer system, housed in the specially adapted skull of an aardvark. The brain will be your contribution, of course. We won't need your actual head."

"Say what??!!"

"Come along, Mr. Giblet It's time for your amalgamation."

Slitherquick coiled around me and constricted, dragging me kicking and screaming to his laboratory. He strapped me to a gurney and wired me to the computer and the aardvark. Beakers filled with bubbling, fizzing green shit wafted fumes that reeked like liquefied decomp strained through dirty, wet socks. Conductor rods arced electricity from positive to negative, humming so loud it rattled the fillings in my teeth. Slitherquick cackled hysterically and put a pair of goggles over his Don Knotts bug-eyes.

He finally threw the switch, and a blinding supernova filled the room. The computer, the aardvark, and I glowed like Chernobyl. I thought my retinas had melted; then I passed out.

When I awoke, Slitherquick removed the straps holding me to the gurney. I sat up slowly, still a little dizzy. But man, I was hungry and so thirsty. He brought me some water and a bowl of food. I sucked down enough water to sink a battleship; then I dipped my snout into the food bowl and nearly choked to death inhaling a bunch of ants down the wrong pipe.

Just in case you're wondering, it doesn't matter which pipe they go down, ants taste like ass. But having a snout isn't all bad. There's a hot little Jessica Alba-honeybee-hippo mix I wouldn't mind snuffling. Know what I mean?

Besides, it's all good. Just between us, stock for Particularis is rising through the roof. The smart money will go all in. I'm Gordon Giblet, and you could say I have the inside track on this. Trust me. The world is headed for amalgamation—one molecule at a time.

The Truths That Set You Free

Near as I could figure, when I was ten, there were three kinds of Baptists in Harlan – the 'singers', the 'wailers', and the 'charmers'.

The singers at First Kentucky Baptist, on Elm Street, wore robes, sang snappy tunes and clapped their hands. My family'd been singers since God split Adams's rib. The wailers at the Holy Word Church, on Cherry Street, prayed with 'new' tongues. I wasn't sure what happened to their old tongues when the new ones showed up, but it didn't matter none, 'cause my friend, Tyson, (whose family'd been wailers since Moses was a child), spoke to me with his old tongue. Mostly. 'Cause when he did commence to wailing, I'd slap him up side his head.

"Why'd you go and do that, Ennis?" he'd ask.

I'd tell him, "Everybody knows if you want saving, you sing— making a joyful noise unto the Lord. You don't go wailing crazy mumbo-jumbo. Jesus'll think your nuts."

Though we tussled over which one of us was headed for the Promised Land, neither of us understood the third kind of Baptist, the 'charmers' at the Heavenly Tabernacle on Pine Street. A strange, mystical lot they were, taking up poisonous snakes. The notion of Jesus and serpents together created a powerful curiosity in Tyson and me. We hankered to see such a glorious spectacle. Sure enough, we got our chance come Pentecost Sunday, in '38, when Harlan held its Holy Ghost Revival.

Each congregation had its own booth, and reeled in potential converts with the likes of Mercy Pickens' "First Baptist Fried Chicken", Granny Baker's, "Holy Word Corn Fritters", and Mrs. Reverend Sykes', "Heavenly Tabernacle Cobbler". But best of all, Reverend Sykes, our resident snake charmer, held his "Salvation Show".

Tyson and I sampled all the vittles', our faces berry stained from ear to ear. Only after we'd licked our plates clean, did Tyson's start his mischief. "Last one to the snake tent's a yellow-belly!"

We ran like we was bein' chased by the devil himself, to the corner of Pine and Main, stopping just before we reached the snake tent, to admire the whitewashed shanty where Reverend Sykes kept his serpents between services. It'd seen better days; its gutters hanging down, and windows boarded over, but one day, in a fit of ecstasy, he'd painted a message from God across the side of it. 'Speak the truth, even if your voice shakes.'

Powerful words, we reckoned, and worthy of preserving that ramshackle shanty; prompting us to give it a brief, but reverent nod before we snuck underneath the backside of Reverend Sykes tent.

The reverend preached loud enough to be heard clear across Harlan County. He sermonized on perdition, and the wages of sin; called forth the sick and the lame, lay on his hands, and then healed them with the power of the Holy Spirit, in Jesus' name. Amen! Hallelujah! There was singing and dancing, and the jabbering of new tongues, all together under one tent. When we were so transfixed we'd nearly forgotten why we'd come, he brought out the snakes; poisonous vipers that raced over his body like floodwaters through a riverbed.

When the show was over, I wasn't sure who was more exhausted, us or Reverend Sykes, but Tyson said he knew one thing for sure. "If he can charm snakes, so can we."

****

Every Hazard youngin', over six-years-old, knew how to find snakes. We just went where we was told not to, and put our hands in places our mommas made us swear we never would.

In no time, a den of rattlers, beneath a rock ledge, shook their tails to discourage us.

Tyson reached for the ledge. I snatched his hand.

"This don't feel right. Let's just go home." I said.

"You gots to believe, Ennis! Like Reverend Sykes told us. 'They shall take up serpents, and if they drink any deadly thing, it shall not hurt them.' Snakes can't hurt true believers, and Jesus knows I believe. He won't let them hurt me any more than He let them hurt the reverend."

His hand crept under the ledge, slow and easy, feeling its way. "Got one!" he whispered.

I held my breath. His arm eased back, slow as a slug.

"See?" he said, smiling to beat the band. "Nothing to it." He turned to show me the rattler, and never saw the strike that came from beneath the ledge. Fangs sunk deep into his neck; venom spewed like liquid fire.

"Tyson!" I screamed. He didn't answer. He just looked surprised and crumpled to the ground.

I stomped the head of the snake that bit him, and the one he'd been holding, too. He weighed more than me, but I hauled him across my shoulder, and stumbled toward home, crying and praying with every fall.

"Don' take him, God! You don't need him. I do. He's my friend. Please, help me, Jesus!"

It was pitch black when they found me in the woods, clutching Tyson's cold, dead body.

Jesus had forsaken us. I was sure I'd never believe again.

But not two weeks later, something happened that sent me to Tyson's grave with a hard truth that needed telling; a truth so hard that it pained my throat coming out.

"Ain't no easy way to say this, Tyson, so I'll just come on out with it. Reverend Sykes run off with the congregation's coffers." I sucked in some air before I spit out the rest. "He was milkin' them show snakes, too, Tyson; that's how come he never got sick when he got bit. It wasn't God let us down – it was that lying, no account, bible thumpin' huckster. Just thought you should know. Rest easy now. I reckon I'll be seeing you some day."

Tyson knew I wouldn't wail for him, but I did sing, "Amazing Grace". My tears began to dry, and when the lump in my throat eased some, I told him what I'd learned. Sometimes, it's the charmers are the snakes.

And sometimes, it's the hardest truths that set you free.

Mary Ann Back

Mary Ann lives in Mason, Ohio, with her husband, Pete and her beloved dog, Max. She is a Pushcart Prize nominee and was awarded the 2009 Bilbo Award for creative writing by Thomas More College. The characters she creates are often disreputable and not to be trusted. She kicks them to the curb every chance she gets when some unwitting publisher agrees to take them off her hands.

Acknowledgments and Prepublication

I wish to thank my friends at Zoetrope's Flash Factory, too numerous to mention, as well as those at Write Stuff Extreme, Antonio Diggs, Will Hahn, Katharina Gerlach and Mary Baader Kaley for their countless reviews and sage advice. Special thanks goes out to Robert M. Burdick, for being my most merciless critic, to the late Janet Joering, for a lifetime of correcting my grammatical errors, and last, but certainly not least, to Harry R. Burdick, Jr. who has my undying gratitude for technical support in all things related to guns, guts, and gore.

I also wish to thank the following publications where these pieces first appeared:

Prime Cut	*A Twist of Noir*	Nov 2011
Lola	*A Twist of Noir*	Nov 2011
Girls' Night Out	*A Twist of Noir*	Feb 2013
Aces and Alibis	*Infective Ink*	May 2012
A Different Shade of Death	*Bete Noire*	July 2011
The Chamber	*Kazka Press*	Oct 2012
Secrets	*Write to Meow*	Nov 2014
The Devil's Due	*Daily Love*	Jan 2013
Mr. Boogens	*Eclectic Flash*	April 2010
Mr. Robbins Goes for a Walk	*Flashshot*	2010
The Transmogrification of Gordon Giblett		
	Apollo's Lyre	*Apr 2012*
The Goddess of War	*365 Tomorrows*	May 2012
The Good Life	*Flashes in the Dark*	Mar 2011
Stiff Willy	*Flash Fiction Funny*	Sept 2014
Extraordinary Moments	*Ni Bona Na Coroin*	May 2014
Promises to Keep	*Apollo's Lyre*	Dec 2011
The Pecking Order	*Short Story America*	May 2010

Sadie's Choice	*Thomas More Anthology*	June 2009
Sometimes	*Loyalhanna Review*	July 2011
The Summer of My Father	*Loyalhanna Review*	July 2009
The Prodigal	*Hellroaring Review*	Jan 2013

Dead Reckoning